HARLEQUIN® Presents

Welcome to the September 2008 collection of Harlequin Presents!

This month, be sure to read favorite author Penny Jordan's *Virgin for the Billionaire's Taking*, in which virginal Keira is whisked off to the exotic world of handsome Jay! Michelle Reid brings you a fabulous tale of a ruthless Italian's convenient bride in *The De Santis Marriage*, while Carol Marinelli's gorgeous tycoon wants revenge on innocent Caitlyn in *Italian Boss, Ruthless Revenge*. And don't miss the final story in Carole Mortimer's brilliant trilogy THE SICILIANS, *The Sicilian's Innocent Mistress!* Abby Green brings you the society wedding of the year in *The Kouros Marriage Revenge*, and in Chantelle Shaw's *At The Sheikh's Bidding*, Erin's life is changed forever when she discovers her adopted son is heir to a desert kingdom!

Also this month, new author Heidi Rice delivers a sizzling, sexy boss in *The Tycoon's Very Personal Assistant*, and in Ally Blake's *The Magnate's Indecent Proposal*, an ordinary girl is faced with a millionaire who's way out of her league. Enjoy!

We'd love to hear what you think about Harlequin Presents. E-mail us at Presents@hmb.co.uk or join in the discussions at www.iheartpresents.com and www.sensationalromance.blogspot.com, where you'll also find more information about books and authors!

Even if at times work is rather boring, there is one person making the office a whole lot more interesting: the boss!

Dark and dangerous, alpha and powerful, rich and ruthless… He's in control, he knows what he wants and he's going to get it! He's tall, handsome, breathtakingly attractive. And there's one outcome that's never in doubt— the heroines of these sparky, supersexy stories will be

Undressed
BY THE BOSS

From sensible suits…into satin sheets!

A brand-new miniseries from Harlequin Presents!

Heidi Rice

THE TYCOON'S VERY PERSONAL ASSISTANT

Undressed
BY THE BOSS

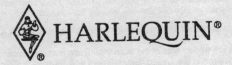

HARLEQUIN®

TORONTO • NEW YORK • LONDON
AMSTERDAM • PARIS • SYDNEY • HAMBURG
STOCKHOLM • ATHENS • TOKYO • MILAN • MADRID
PRAGUE • WARSAW • BUDAPEST • AUCKLAND

ISBN-13: 978-0-373-12761-0
ISBN-10: 0-373-12761-8

THE TYCOON'S VERY PERSONAL ASSISTANT

First North American Publication 2008.

All about the author...
Heidi Rice

HEIDI RICE was born and bred—and still lives—
in London, England. She has two boys who love
to bicker, a wonderful husband who, luckily for
everyone, has loads of patience, and a supportive
and ever-growing British/French/Irish/American
family. As much as Heidi adores "the Big Smoke,"
she also loves America, and every two years
or so she and her best friend leave hubby and
kids behind and *Thelma and Louise* it across
the States for a couple of weeks (although
they always leave out the driving-off-a-cliff bit).
She's been a film buff since her early teens
and a romance junkie for almost as long. She
indulged her first love by being a film reviewer
for the past ten years. Then, two years ago, she
decided to spice up her life by writing romance.
Discovering the fantastic sisterhood of romance
writers (both published and unpublished)
in Britain and America made it a wild and
wonderful journey to her first Harlequin novel,
and she's looking forward to many more to
come. Heidi loves to hear from readers,
and you can contact her through her Web site
at www.heidi-rice.com.

To Chessie Welker, my American dialogue coach,
for telling me that rubbers went out in the fifties
and rich guys don't drink cheap beer!

CHAPTER ONE

'I TOLD YOU I'm not a working girl.' Kate Denton shifted on the stiff leather chair and shot the man sitting on the other side of the mahogany desk her don't-mess-with-me look. Jet-lagged, shaken and as good as naked under the hotel robe she had on, Kate knew the look wasn't one of her best.

He didn't reply. The insistent tap of his pen against the desk blotter seemed deafening in the silence. Bright Vegas sunlight shone through the wall of glass to his right and cast his face into shadow, making it impossible to tell his reaction.

Oh, goody, Kate thought grimly. After the most humiliating experience of my entire life, I get interrogated by a hotel manager with a God complex.

Apprehension slithered around in Kate's stomach like a hyperactive snake. Why on earth had she demanded to see the hotel manager in the first place? It had seemed like a good idea when the concierge had started making noises about calling the police, but once she'd been whisked up to the penthouse suite of offices and ushered in here, she'd started having serious doubts. The guy wasn't behaving like any hotel manager she'd ever met.

She felt more intimidated now than before.

Obviously hotel managers had a much higher profile in the States. This guy's workspace would have made the Oval

Office look tacky. A lake of luxurious blue carpeting flowed to floor-to-ceiling windows, showcasing the hotel's enviable position towering over the Las Vegas Strip. The view wasn't the only thing giving Kate vertigo. The room was so big it accommodated a separate seating area with three deluxe leather sofas, and Kate had recognised the striking canvas on the far wall as that of a modern artist whose work now went for millions. She'd also noticed the guy had not one but three secretaries standing guard outside.

No wonder he had a God complex.

'A working girl? You mean a hooker?' His deep voice rumbled out at last, sending an annoying shiver of awareness up Kate's spine. 'I don't recall saying I thought you were a hooker, honey.'

Kate heard the hint of amusement and her jaw tensed. 'Who gave you permission to call me honey?' she said, grateful for the crisp note of condescension in her voice.

'I don't need permission,' he replied dryly, 'when the lady in question was trying to break down a door in my hotel wearing nothing but a bra and thong.'

Kate swallowed. Okay, there was that.

'It's not a thong. I have proper knickers on,' she blurted out, and then winced.

The memory of getting caught by the bell captain and bundled into a robe flooded back to her. Embarrassment scorched her cheeks. The fact she had something slightly more substantial than a thong covering her bottom suddenly didn't seem all that relevant. That she'd mentioned it to *him* was mortifying. She'd yet to get a proper look at the guy and already he knew far too much about her underwear.

The metronome taps of his pen interrupted her thoughts. 'Proper panties or not, you were causing a disturbance.'

The heat in Kate's cheeks soared. What was this guy's problem? She was the one who'd been manhandled. So she'd raised her voice and kicked the door a little, but wouldn't anyone who got stranded in a hotel corridor practically naked?

'I was trying to get back into the room.'

'Yeah, but it wasn't your room, was it?' He leaned forward, propping his elbows on the desk, and the sunlight illuminated his features at last.

Kate's heart pulsed hard. Hooded green eyes studied her out of a tanned face that was quite simply dazzling in its masculine beauty. Sharp black brows, chiselled cheeks and short dark hair that curled around his ears only added to the firepower. Even with his face carefully devoid of expression, the guy might as well have had a huge neon sign over his head flashing the word 'irresistible' at her.

From the way he was watching her, she wondered if he was waiting for her to swoon. She tightened the tie on the robe, absolutely determined not to start drooling.

Luckily for her, she was currently immune to the alpha male of the species.

'It *was* my room, or at least it was supposed to be,' she said, annoyed by the quake in her voice. She wrapped her arms round her waist, far too aware of the air-conditioned breeze chilling her bare legs.

His gaze swept over her and Kate felt the throb of response. All right, maybe not completely immune.

'You're not registered here.' His emerald eyes shifted back to hers. 'Mr Rocastle, who *is* the registered guest, has made a complaint against you. So, why don't you tell me why I shouldn't just kick you out in your proper panties?'

There it was again, the tell-tale lift in his voice. Kate went rigid. Was he making fun of her?

Andrew Rocastle had duped her, practically assaulted her and then humiliated her into the bargain. And now this guy thought it was funny. When had this become stomp-all-over-Kate day?

'It's not my fault Mr Rocastle didn't put my name on the

registration card when he checked us in this morning. I thought he'd booked us separate rooms,' she ground out, angry all over again at Andrew's underhanded attempt at a seduction. 'And anyway, I don't have to explain myself to you. None of this is any of your business. You're a hotel manager, not my mother.'

Zack Boudreaux's eyebrow winged up. For such a little thing, she sure had a big mouth. He didn't consider himself arrogant, but women were usually a lot nicer to him. He'd certainly never encountered this level of hostility before.

In the normal course of events, he wouldn't even know about this type of minor disturbance, let alone be asked to deal with it. But with The Phoenix's manager on vacation for the day and his deputy on a training programme, the concierge had referred the matter up to Zack's PA. He'd heard the commotion in the outer office and buzzed the woman in out of curiosity. Truth be told, after clearing his calendar for the rest of the week in preparation for his trip to California, he'd found himself with nothing to do for the first time in close to ten years and he was bored.

One thing was for sure, the minute this feisty little firecracker had waltzed into his office wrapped in her bathrobe and a very bad attitude, he hadn't been bored any more.

He knew it was perverse, but for some weird reason he found her sassy comebacks entertaining. Imagining her in the corridor without the bathrobe was doing the rest.

'I don't manage this hotel,' he said. 'I own it, as well as two others in the South West.'

'Bully for you,' she shot back, but the statement lacked impact when he spotted the flicker of panic cross her face.

'And anything that happens in my place is my business.' His gaze remained steady on hers. 'I make a point of it.' He kept his voice firm. He hadn't made a fortune at poker in his youth by showing his cards too early. He didn't want to let her off the hook just yet. She *had* caused a disturbance and he was intrigued enough to want to know why.

'Maybe you could make a point of getting my clothes back for me, then,' she snapped.

Zack's lips twitched as she glared at him. With her blonde hair haloing around her head in haphazard wisps, her full lips puckered in a defiant pout and her round turquoise eyes bright with temper, she looked cute and mad and sexy as hell. Kind of like a pixie with an anger-management problem.

His lips curved before he could stop them.

Her round baby-blues narrowed dangerously. 'Excuse me, but do you think this is funny?' The clear, precise English accent made his pulse spike.

Her voice should have reminded him of weak tea and pompous aristocrats—the two things he'd hated most during the years he'd spent in London as a teenager—but it had a smoky, seductive edge that made him think of rumpled bed sheets and warm fragrant flesh instead.

He cleared his throat, and stifled the grin. 'Funny's not the word I'd use,' he said.

She tugged hard on the lapels of the thick robe, hastily covering the hint of red lace.

His eyes rose as he acknowledged the quick punch of lust. 'Don't worry, you'll get your clothes back,' he said. 'But first I want to know how you and Rocastle are connected and what he did to make you want to cause my hotel criminal damage.'

Kate jerked one stiff shoulder, feeling trapped but trying desperately for nonchalance. 'I'm his PA, or at least I was.' She raised her chin, struggling hard to keep the quiver of nerves out of her voice. 'He wanted to take our association to another level. I didn't. I told him so. End of story,' she said, putting more pomp and circumstance into her accent than a Royal Jubilee.

Maybe if she told this nosy American Adonis that much he'd lose interest and let her leave. The smouldering look he'd given her a moment ago—as if he could see right through the towelling—had not been good for her heart rate. And it wasn't doing a great deal for her peace of mind, either.

How could she possibly find the man attractive? He might look good enough to eat. But, from what she'd seen so far, he was an over-confident, insensitive jerk. Surely she'd dealt with enough of those today to give her indigestion. So he owned the hotel. So what? That hardly gave him the right to have a laugh at her expense.

'I see,' he said in the same wry monotone, as if she were sitting here in her underwear for his personal amusement. 'And you told him this without your clothes on?'

'I was about to take a shower. I didn't know he'd booked us into the same suite.' Tears of frustration stung Kate's eyes, his careless comment bringing the whole sordid experience back in vivid colour. She blinked furiously, determined not to cry.

How could she have been so stupid?

If only she'd figured out Andrew's real reason for employing her sooner she might have been able to salvage a tiny bit of her pride. But she'd been so eager to impress him, to prove she was worthy of the opportunity he was offering her, she'd made a total fool of herself. That she had been idiotic enough to trust Andrew hurt more than anything else, even more than finding herself in the corridor in her bra and knickers when she'd informed Andrew exactly where he could shove his proposition.

She swallowed past the boulder in her throat. 'I still don't see how this is any of your business.' Her fingers clutched the robe, now wrapped so tightly around her she could barely breathe. 'Are you going to press charges or not?'

The two-second wait for his reply felt like two decades. She was sure he knew it.

He dropped his pen on the desk and steepled his fingers. 'I guess not,' he said at last.

Relief coursed through her. 'Thank you,' she said, trying to sound as if she meant it. At least he hadn't made her beg. 'I'll be off, then.' She stood up.

'Hold it, we're not through yet,' he said.

To her dismay, he stood up too and walked round the desk towards her.

Lord, he was tall. Long and lean with a very impressive pair of shoulders filling out his pricey linen shirt. She was a perfectly respectable five feet four herself but had to tilt her head back as he approached. She curled her toes into the soft carpeting and fought the desire to drop into the chair. She wasn't about to give him even more of a height advantage.

'I don't see what else there is to discuss,' she said, despising the tremble in her voice.

'Oh, I don't know,' he said, slowly. 'How about—?' He broke off as the phone rang. 'Stay put,' he said, pointing at her as if she were a trained beagle. He leaned across the desk and grabbed the phone. 'Boudreaux,' he barked into the receiver.

Kate bristled but did as she was told. Infuriatingly enough, it occurred to her she would need Mr Sex God's permission to get back into Andrew's room to get her clothes.

'Uh-huh.' He nodded, obviously engrossed by whatever was being said on the other end of the line. 'Did he say where he was going?' He listened some more, his gaze fixing on her face. His eyes hardened and his beautifully sculpted lips flattened into a thin line. 'What about ID?' he said into the phone, sounding annoyed. He raked his hand through his hair and cursed under his breath. The short dark waves fell back into place perfectly. He must have spent a small fortune on that haircut, Kate thought resentfully.

'Sure. No, don't bother. I'll figure it out.' He slapped the phone back in its cradle, nodded at her chair. 'You better sit down.'

Irritation edged his voice but there was a touch of warmth in those remarkable eyes that hadn't been there before. The knot of anxiety in Kate's stomach tightened. She sat in the chair, heard the leather creak as she pressed her knees together. What now?

Leaning on the corner of the desk, he crossed his long legs at the ankle. He was so close, Kate could smell the intimate scent of soap and man. She concentrated on the perfect crease in his trousers, trying to ignore the way the expensive fabric stretched across powerful thigh muscles.

'Rocastle's checked out,' he said above her.

Kate's chin jerked up. The knowledge she'd never have to see the contemptible worm again had her breath gushing out in an audible puff. Maybe now she could start putting this whole humiliating business behind her. 'If you could give me a key to the room, I'll get dressed and leave, too,' she said.

She'd expected him to look overjoyed at the prospect of her departure. He didn't, he looked pained. 'It's not going to be that easy.' He crossed his arms over his chest, making the rolled up sleeves of his shirt tighten across his biceps. 'He took your luggage.'

'What? *All* of it?'

He rocked back and nodded. 'Everything but your ID.'

'But why?' Kate's mouth hung open.

He uncrossed his arms and braced his hands on the desk behind him, tilting his upper body forwards. 'Rocastle said to tell you you're fired and he's taking your stuff and cashing your ticket home to cover his expenses.'

'But...' Panic clawed up the back of her throat. She gulped it down.

How could Andrew do this? He must know he was leaving her stranded.

'But he can't do that. Those are my things.' Indignation seared her insides, but beneath it was the bitter sting of fear. Surely this couldn't be happening. 'How will I get back to London?'

Zack had expected her to get mad again. In fact he'd been looking forward to seeing her eyes spark with temper. But when he saw confusion and desperation on her face instead, her situation didn't seem all that funny any more. Maybe there was more going on here than a lover's spat.

Her boyfriend or boss or whatever he was sounded like a real piece of work. Maybe the girl was nuttier than a jar of peanut butter, but there was something cold and calculating about the way the guy had cleared out the suite and left his girlfriend in a strange city, in a strange hotel in nothing but her underwear.

She ducked her head and stared down at her lap. Her fingers clutched together, the knuckles whitening as she took an uneven breath. When her head came up, she didn't look mad, she looked devastated. He noticed the rim of purple surrounding the deep blue of her irises. The hint of moisture in her eyes accentuated the unusual colour. She sniffed and straightened in her chair, but no tears fell. He felt an unfamiliar constriction in his chest that he recognised as admiration.

'You want me to call the cops?' he asked, figuring that was the logical next step.

She shook her head, thrust out her pointy little chin. 'Could I ask you a favour?'

His chest loosened. Here it came. She was going to ask him for money. It didn't surprise him. She was in a fix and from her accent and her flaky behaviour so far he figured she must be the rich, pampered daughter of some stuck-up Brit. He doubted she'd ever had to fend for herself in her entire life. Still, he felt oddly disappointed. 'Fire away,' he said.

'Would you give me a job?'

'A job?' Was she serious?

'Yes, I've done some bar-tending and waitressing and I've got lots of experience as a chambermaid.'

'You've scrubbed johns? You're kidding me?' He could see the Queen of England doing it sooner than he could imagine *her* doing it.

'No, I'm not,' she said, sounding affronted.

'Have you got a work visa?' he asked, although he didn't know why. He didn't want her tending bar, or scrubbing johns—it just didn't seem right somehow.

'Yes, I have dual nationality. I was born in New York.'

'Right.' Dumb question. 'Look, we could work something out for you if you want, but you don't need a job. All you need do is get the cops to have a talk with your boyfriend and—'

'He's not my boyfriend,' she interrupted.

'Whatever he is, he can't steal your stuff.'

'I'm not going to go grovelling to the police or anyone else,' she said. 'They're only clothes. As far as I'm concerned Andrew can keep them. And he paid for the plane ticket, so he can keep that too.'

'Aren't you forgetting something?'

Annoyance flashed, but she kept her gaze locked on his. 'What's that?'

'You can't tend bar in your underwear.'

She blinked, then looked away. The slight tremor in her shoulders made his chest constrict again.

He felt as if he'd just kicked a puppy.

Kate twisted her hands in her lap. 'You may have a point there,' she said, trying to sound flippant as she forced her gaze back to his. The fighting spirit seeped out of her, though, as she endured his long, steady stare. Did he still think her situation was funny—or, worse, pathetic?

She couldn't get the police involved. Her pride wouldn't

allow it. She'd rather prance down The Strip stark naked than see Andrew again. But she didn't have more than twenty pounds in her purse. When she'd arrived at work yesterday morning she hadn't expected to be whisked off to Las Vegas on a 'business trip' by her boss. She didn't have a job any more. Her one credit card was maxed out. None of her friends had the sort of money she'd need to get home. And she'd sooner amputate a limb than ask her father for help.

She'd been surviving on her own since she was seventeen years old. Kate squared her shoulders, tried to control the panic making her hands shake. She'd got herself into this predicament. She'd just have to get herself out again.

The knowledge she'd have to throw herself on the mercy of the man in front of her made her stomach hurt. She hated to be indebted to anyone. Especially someone like him. Someone so rich, self-assured and domineering. But her pride had taken so many hits already today, how much damage could one more do?

Kate curled her hands into fists. 'I know it's a bit cheeky, but if I start work tomorrow could you give me an advance on my salary?'

Zack could see the request had cost her. The colour had washed out of her already pale face and she sat so rigidly on the edge of her chair it was a miracle she didn't topple off onto the floor. Even so, the urge to take that defeated look out of her eyes surprised him.

He wasn't the kind of guy who rescued damsels in distress. Especially not damsels in distress with enough attitude to make Joan Rivers look like Snow White.

But try as he might, he couldn't quite shake the desire to help her out.

Maybe it was that combination of guts and vulnerability. Or maybe it was just her honesty. She could have used her looks, could have resorted to the usual feminine wiles, but she hadn't. He had to give her points for that.

'The suite's paid up till the day after tomorrow,' he lied smoothly, knowing Rocastle would have got a refund on the booking. 'I'll get the concierge to let you in and we'll send up some clothes.'

Surprise and relief flittered across her face, but then a wary look came into her eyes. Small white teeth raked over her bottom lip. 'I'm not…' Whatever she was going to say she stopped herself. 'That's very generous of you.' She hesitated again, but only for a moment, before she stood up. 'I'm sorry if I was rude earlier.' She sighed, the little gush of breath making the hairs on the back of his neck stand up. 'It's been a difficult day.'

'No problem.' He shrugged, feeling a slither of guilt for having baited her. 'No harm done.'

She held out her hand. 'My name's Kate, by the way. Kate Denton.'

Kate. Sweet, simple and kind of plain. It didn't suit her one bit he decided as he gripped her fingers.

'Zack Boudreaux. Good to meet you, Kate,' he said, surprised to realise it was true. He felt a slight jolt run through her before she pulled her hand out of his grasp. 'What size are you?' he asked, glancing down at her figure. It was impossible to tell beneath all that terry cloth.

'I'm an American size eight.'

The tint of colour that hit her cheeks amused him. Good to know she wasn't entirely indifferent to him.

'I'll start work first thing tomorrow,' she continued, all businesslike.

He smiled.

'I'll probably be up at the crack of dawn anyway because of the jet lag,' she said, rushing the words.

Yeah, he was definitely making her nervous. The thought

pleased him. 'The personnel manager will be in touch,' he said, with no intention of following through.

No way was he giving her a job. He'd get the concierge to give her a couple hundred bucks, send her up some clothes and organise a plane ticket home. It was the least he could do for the entertainment value.

'Don't forget to take the cost of the clothes out of my salary,' she said over her shoulder as she turned to go. His gaze drifted down her back as she walked to the door. Her bare feet sank into the carpet, making her seem almost childlike. But then he noticed the stiff set of her shoulders and the seductive sway of her hips through the shapeless knee-length garment.

She was quite something, he thought as the door clicked closed behind her. He was going to miss her. Which was dumb, considering he'd only just met her and during that time she hadn't exactly been coming on to him.

He sat at his desk and picked up his pen to begin jotting a 'to-do' list for his trip to California at the end of the week.

Twenty minutes later Zack still sat at the desk, pen in hand, without having put a single solitary item on the list.

'Hell!' He ripped the sheet of paper off the jotter, balled it up and sent it flying into the trash. No wonder he couldn't think—a certain blue-eyed pixie with blonde hair and an attitude problem kept popping into his head.

Why did Kate Denton fascinate him? She was pretty, but she was hardly his type. He liked his women sleek, sophisticated and most of all predictable. On the evidence of their brief encounter, Little Miss Proper Knickers was about as predictable as Lady Luck.

He stood up, dumping the pen on the desk, and rubbed the back of his neck.

Maybe that was it.

Since he'd given up gambling ten years ago, invested all

his time and money into building his hotel empire, the women he'd dated had looked beautiful, behaved impeccably and never once made him work for what he wanted. They'd certainly never talked back to him, challenged him the way Kate Denton had. How many years was it since he'd felt the thrill of the chase?

He'd once thrived on the rush of adrenaline that came with the turn of the cards, and he'd transferred all of that drive, all of that ambition into his quest to change his life—to drag it out of the shadowy world he'd grown up in of gambling dens and back-alley casinos. At thirty-two, after ten long years of hard work, he'd been featured on the cover of *Fortune* magazine, was ranked as one of America's top-ten entrepreneurs by *Newsweek*. He owned a beach house in the Bahamas and a Lear jet. And The Phoenix franchise had evolved from a small casino hotel in Vegas into the most vibrant, sought-after hospitality brand in the South West.

He strolled over to the office's window. Resting his hand on the glass, he looked down. Twenty floors below, the afternoon sunlight laid The Strip bare. Without the cloaking spell of nighttime, the glamour of a million colourful neon lights, the famous street looked jaded, its seedy underbelly plain for everyone to see. This was a town that had been built on the promise of an easy buck, the promise of a quick green-backed fix to life's woes. It was a promise that could destroy lives—it had almost destroyed his—and he'd decided over the last decade that, if he was ever going to truly escape his past, he couldn't be a party to that promise any more. He'd already expanded The Phoenix brand into New Mexico and Arizona with huge success and now, at last, he was ready to sell his flagship hotel and get the hell out of Vegas—and the casino business—for good.

He let his arm drop back to his side. From what Monty, his best friend and business manager, had said in his call from California yesterday, Zack was only a few weeks away from taking that last crucial step into the light. He didn't really need any distractions right now.

But with his dream about to be realised, why did he still feel as jaded as the city he had come to despise?

After his run-in with the feisty, fascinating Kate Denton and her big mouth, it occurred to him that fulfilling his long-term business plans was only going to solve part of the problem. His personal life needed a makeover too. During the last ten years he'd allowed himself to drift through a series of lazy and unfulfilling affairs. What was that old saying about all work and no play? He had a few days off for the first time in, well, for ever. Surely there'd never be a better time to play.

Zack turned to stare at the empty chair opposite his desk. Yeah, Kate Denton would be one heck of a distraction. But she'd also be a challenge. And he always thrived on challenges.

As Zack picked up the phone, he pictured her captivating face, the wild blonde hair, those striking sky-blue eyes, her plump, kissable Cupid's bow mouth, and didn't try to deny the sharp tug of sexual desire.

Volatile or not, she'd be worth the effort, he'd lay odds on it.

As he tapped out the concierge's number Zack let the heady mix of adrenaline and arousal pulse through his veins. Damned if he didn't feel better already. More alive, more excited than he had in years.

They might only have a couple of days to enjoy each other, but he planned to see a whole lot more of Miss Kate Denton and her 'proper knickers'.

CHAPTER TWO

CONTRARY TO POPULAR opinion, Kate didn't believe crying ever made anyone feel better. In her experience, crying made you feel rubbish—and look even worse—and now she had conclusive proof, staring back at her out of the bathroom mirror.

Dabbing at her puffy, red-rimmed eyes with a damp tissue, Kate willed the tears to stop. She'd been at it for over twenty minutes and it was giving her a blistering headache. She wasn't even sure what she was crying about any more.

Yes, Andrew had been a creep, but she should have seen that one coming. She'd convinced herself his interest in her had stemmed from admiration and mutual respect. But she should have known better. Since when did guys admire and respect women like her? Women who had an opinion and voiced it. She should have guessed something was wrong as soon as Andrew said he liked her sassiness. No man ever had before, starting with her father.

Kate watched her brow furrow in the mirror, felt the wave of sadness and inadequacy that always accompanied thoughts of her father.

James Dalton Asquith III had only wanted her mother for one thing—and he'd certainly never wanted a daughter. When he'd been forced to take her in after her mother's death, Kate had tried desperately to please him, to be who he wanted her to be. At seventeen she'd finally accepted the truth—that the fault lay with him, not her—which made it all the more galling that in some small, forgotten corner of her heart his rejection still hurt.

Running away from home all those years ago had been the smartest thing she'd ever done. A liberating experience that had made her realise she didn't need her father's approval, or his charity. She took a slow, calming breath and gave her cheeks one last swipe with a fresh tissue from the vanity unit.

Finally figuring out what a heel Andrew was could well be the next smartest. She breathed out again, glad not to hear a single hitch. She'd cried her last tear over Andrew Rocastle—and her father for that matter.

She screwed the tissue up and shoved it in the pocket of the bathrobe. Flushing the toilet, she walked out into the living area of the suite. Her stomach knotted as she spotted the soft leather sofa where Andrew had been sitting when she'd walked out of the bathroom in her underwear.

Surprise had quickly given way to fury when she'd discovered what Andrew had in mind for their so-called business trip. Didn't she realise where their relationship was leading? he'd said. As if she'd been a party to his ridiculous fantasies. Frankly she'd been more turned on by one look from Zack Boudreaux, the hotel tycoon from planet sexy, than she had by all Andrew's attention in the last few weeks. He'd accused her of sending him mixed messages. Tears of humiliation clogged up her throat as she recalled how he'd shoved her out of the suite while she'd been giving him another message entirely, at top volume.

Kate sniffed the tears back and gave a weary sigh, pushing the aggravating memory to the far reaches of her mind. She had other, more pressing problems to deal with now. She was back at square one, right where she'd been when she'd walked out on her father and his indifference ten years ago—broke and 'scrubbing johns' for a living. Except this time she was doing it thousands of miles from home with a distinct lack of clothing.

She plumped herself down on the sofa.

At least she'd learned something from this situation. Never trust anyone, and don't kid yourself. If something looks too good to be true, it is.

Picking up the TV remote she switched on the huge plasma screen that took up the opposite wall of the suite.

Perma-pressed chat show hosts and adverts for haemorrhoid cream flicked by as she trolled through the channels. Her thumb stopped dead as a raunchy scene in a daytime soap opera flashed onto the screen. A buxom blonde appeared to be Unibonded to a hairless muscle-bound male torso. Kate tilted her head, trying to figure out where the chest ended and the blonde began.

'For Pete's sake, isn't that a bit much for ten in the morning?' she said out loud as the camera lifted and the couple proceeded to suck each other's faces off.

Then the guy came up for air. He droned a series of banal lines but all Kate noticed was the jewel-green tone of his eyes. It reminded her of someone.

She tucked her legs up under her, refusing to acknowledge the tingling sensation between her thighs. Her thumb jerked down on the channel-change button, but not before she'd had the errant thought that Zack Boudreaux's eyes were a much more compelling shade of green and that she'd bet her knickers the hotel tycoon had hair on his chest.

Of course, once she'd conjured up the picture of Boudreaux's naked torso in her mind she couldn't get it out again. No matter how many channels she surfed through.

Eventually she gave up and turned the telly off. Throwing the zapper down on the glass-topped coffee-table, she grasped her ankles and willed herself to calm down. Hadn't she just promised herself she wasn't going to put herself at the mercy of any man again, especially not a man like Zack Boudreaux? The guy had testosterone oozing out of his pores. Not only that, but she'd spent all of twenty minutes in his company and it had taken her about two seconds to realise he was exactly the sort of guy any woman with a single independent thought should stay well away from. A man like him would trample all over you without even realising he was doing it.

Stop thinking about him right this instant, she told herself sharply. Now if she could just get rid of the warm, liquid and completely unprecedented feeling that had settled between her thighs…

Kate's head snapped up at the sharp knock on the door.

'Hi, I'm Michelle.' The pristine young woman standing in the corridor had one of those megawatt sales assistant's smiles pasted on her face. 'I'm from Ella's Boutique downstairs. Mr Boudreaux asked us personally to bring up a selection of clothes for you to look at.'

Kate cursed the guilty flush that spread up her neck at the mention of his name. 'He did?'

'Yeah, he did.' The young woman beamed back and then shuffled into the room wheeling a portable garment rail behind her. A profusion of colours and fabrics hung from it. 'He said for you to pick out as many outfits as you need for your stay with us.'

'Oh.' Kate didn't know what else to say. She'd expected a pair of hotel overalls or something, not a selection of the latest catwalk fashions.

'Would you like me to lay them out for you?'

Kate stared at the rail. 'Um.' She bit her lip. 'No, don't bother.'

Silk dresses vied for position with designer jeans, cashmere sweaters, a Dolce & Gabbana T-shirt. Kate rubbed a satin top between her thumb and forefinger. The cloth was a deep vivid purple, cool and whisper smooth to the touch. Lifting it off the rail, she studied the perfect stitching, the delicately beaded neckline, the way the cloth draped in shimmering waves. She'd never owned a piece of clothing this gorgeous in her life. Or, she imagined, this expensive.

'Why don't they have any price tags?' Kate asked, hooking the purple blouse back onto the rail.

'Oh, well.' The girl's smile faltered as she hesitated. Obviously her customers didn't usually concern themselves with something as mundane as prices. 'You don't need them, ma'am,' she said, brightening again. 'Mr Boudreaux said to charge everything to the hotel.'

Kate gaped at the girl, momentarily struck dumb by Boudreaux's generosity. Then reality intervened. That was ridiculous—he couldn't possibly have intended to give her hundreds of dollars worth of clothing. The boutique staff must have misunderstood. He had probably intended for them to charge the clothes to Kate's hotel room.

'I'd still like to know the prices,' she said, trying not to sound ungracious.

The girl looked confused. 'I guess I could call down to the boutique and get Monica, my supervisor, to itemise them once you've made your selection.'

'All right,' Kate said. Although it wasn't all right. She'd much rather know the prices up front. As beautiful as the clothing was she didn't want to be scrubbing johns in Mr Irresistible's hotel for the rest of her life, which could very well happen if she picked the wrong thing. Most of this stuff would retail in the hundreds, possibly even thousands.

But at the same time Kate didn't want to embarrass herself further by making a big deal of it, and she also didn't want to seem ungrateful. Frankly, she'd been astonished when Boudreaux had offered to help her out in the first place, she didn't want to press her luck.

She opted for the plainest pair of jeans she could find and a simple blue T-shirt with The Phoenix logo on it. At the bottom of the rail was a box with a selection of shoes. Once again, the designs, colours and craftsmanship had her controlling a whimper. She recognised a pair of Fendis and some Manolo Blahniks from the style magazines she loved to paw over at home. She turned to Michelle, who was busy boxing up her selections.

'Do you have any trainers?'

'You don't like the shoes here?' Michelle looked thoroughly crestfallen now.

'Oh, no, it's not that, they're gorgeous. It's just I need something less dressy.'

'Dressy?' The girl glanced at the shoes, her eyebrows lifting. She obviously considered five-hundred-dollar shoes perfectly acceptable for day wear, but to Kate's relief she didn't say it. 'The sportswear store in the hotel forum sells Converse and Nike—is that what you mean?'

'Perfect.' Even with the hotel mark-up, she was sure she could find something for fifty dollars.

The girl's eyes widened, but she nodded. Kate had no doubt at all the shop staff would soon be abuzz with gossip about the dotty English girl in the Sunset Suite with the dress sense of a teenage boy. She forced herself not to care. With the stuff she had she could at least leave the suite—and start work tomorrow—without being indentured for life.

The girl took her shoe size and promised to have a pair sent up to the suite. She wheeled her rail back out the door, but stopped when she got over the threshold. 'Oh, I almost forgot. Mr Boudreaux sent up a package for you.' The girl unclipped a white hotel bag from the end of the rail with an envelope attached to the front. 'I swear, I'd forget my head if it weren't glued to my neck,' she said, giving Kate a nervous smile.

Kate smiled back, or at least she tried to. Why would Boudreaux be sending her packages? Her hand shook ever so slightly as she reached for the bag. 'Thank you.'

'Well…' The girl hesitated. Kate guessed she might be waiting for her to open the package. She wasn't about to oblige. She had no idea what was inside, but the way her luck was going lately she thought it might be bad, like a demand to leave. Maybe he'd changed his mind about helping her out.

'He brought it into the boutique and gave it to me specially,' the girl continued, the awed tone of her voice making it sound as if she thought Boudreaux were the new Messiah.

Kate slung the package under her arm and rubbed her dampening palms on her hotel robe. 'I really appreciate you going to all this trouble. Do tell your supervisor thanks from me, too,' she said, as politely as possible.

Maybe the girl was waiting for a tip? If she was, she was going to be waiting a very long time.

The girl gave a slight hitch of her shoulders. 'No problem, it's all part of the service.' Her eyes flicked to the package one last time. 'Have a nice day.' So saying Michelle took off down the corridor, the clothes-laden rail making a swishing sound on the carpet as she pulled it along behind her.

Kate closed the door and leaned back against it. Why did her knees feel wobbly? She glanced at the flimsy package, which she could have sworn was now throbbing under her arm like a ticking bomb. While she'd been standing in the doorway waiting for the girl to leave it had occurred to her just how dependent she was on Boudreaux's largesse. Sucking in a deep breath, she walked into the room and flung the package on the coffee-table. The white envelope attached to the front had her name written on it in bold black ink. It had to be his handwriting, she thought. The large looping letters and the thick black line slashed under the words seemed to exude confidence, arrogance even—just as he did. She could imagine him writing it with the fountain pen he'd been tapping on his desk, his long tanned fingers moving quickly and efficiently across the paper.

She sighed and sat down. Oh, stop it, you dope. Just open the stupid thing and get it over with. If he'd asked her to leave, she'd leave. He'd honoured the promise about the clothes, which was the main thing. No reason why she couldn't find a job in another hotel now, until she paid him back and earned her airfare home. That the thought of leaving the hotel made her feel a little depressed was simply ridiculous. Why on earth should she care? She wasn't any better off here than she would be anywhere else in Vegas.

She guessed the butterflies jitterbugging in her stomach and the cold fingers of dread flitting up her spine must be the result of exhaustion and her recent emotional trauma, nothing more. She folded her legs and tugged the envelope off the package in one quick, decisive move. Still, as she put her finger into the seam and ripped the envelope open the feeling of dread tightened into an icy fist.

Five crisp new hundred-dollar bills spilled onto her lap. She scooped them up and stared at them. Clutching them in one hand, she unfolded the thick cream paper with the hotel's green and gold letterhead at the top. It took a moment for her eyes to focus on the brief note, scrawled in that same dominant black ink in the middle of the page.

Kate,
Hope you found something to go with those proper knickers.
Meet me for dinner tonight, 8pm in the Rainbow Room.
Z

The signature Z had been slashed across the bottom like the mark of Zorro.

Kate blinked and read the note three more times, but there was still no mention of the five hundred dollars. The feeling of foreboding had gone, but in its place was something much more disturbing. Heat shot into her cheeks and the butterflies in her belly were all burned to a crisp. What was this fixation he seemed to have with her knickers? Why did she find it arousing instead of insulting? And what exactly was the five hundred dollars for?

She didn't want to meet him for dinner tonight. She didn't want to make a fool of herself again, or, worse, come across like someone on the make. But the invitation sounded like an order, and she couldn't afford to annoy him.

She remembered the small package then. The hotel bag had been taped shut. It didn't look as if there was much in it. Undoing the tape she upended the bag and a scrap of lacy crimson satin with a Post-it note stuck to it fell out onto the coffee-table. She picked it up, and pulled the satin thing tight between her fingers.

A thong! Her cheeks blazed and her breath got choppy.

She read the Post-it note: 'These are for you, Kate, in case you want a break from your proper knickers.'

'Why, you cheeky…' Kate was outraged.

But a bubble of something worked its way up her torso. The light and airy feeling fanned out across her chest and a smile she couldn't seem to stop spread across her face.

Then, completely against her will, she began to laugh, for what felt like the first time in a millennium.

CHAPTER THREE

KATE WASN'T LAUGHING when she stepped into the elevator that evening. As the empty car whipped soundlessly up to the nineteenth floor she knew the weightlessness in her stomach had more to do with nerves than gravity.

She studied her reflection in the mirror on the elevator's back wall. At least she didn't look like a vagabond. After a short but fortifying nap, she'd taken one of the hundred-dollar bills Boudreaux had given her and hit The Strip, aware she could hardly wear her Tom Sawyer outfit to the hotel's swankiest restaurant.

She absolutely was not dressing up to impress Boudreaux, but she didn't want to look ridiculous either. Luckily for Kate, she happened to be an expert at styling on a budget. She'd found the vintage blue and gold silk dress in a Salvation Army thrift shop for twenty dollars. It was a little snug around her breasts, showing a bit more cleavage than was probably intended, but otherwise it could have been made for her. The classic hourglass nineteen-fifties styles looked retro, not out of date, she told herself, especially once she added the heeled sandals and clutch purse she'd found on sale at an outlet store on Fremont Street. Kate had never been a shopaholic, she'd never had the finances for it, but she did get a buzz out of co-ordinating the perfect outfit for peanuts. She'd trolled the cosmetics counters at the nearest mall and picked up a sack full of free samples, so even with the headscarf she'd bought to tie up her hair she'd managed to keep her spending under eighty dollars.

Keeping back twenty dollars for emergencies, Kate stuffed the other four hundred dollars Boudreaux had lent her inside her new purse. She pressed it against her belly and peered over her shoulder to get a view of her bum. The tangle of nerves and anticipation eased a little. She looked great. Maybe a bit unusual, but still great. Unfortunately, she didn't feel all that great.

Ever since she'd started getting ready an hour ago, a troop of Morris dancers wearing hobnailed boots had been having a hoedown under her breastbone.

Why did Boudreaux want to have dinner with her?

They hadn't exactly hit it off up to this point. The obvious answer was that he saw in her an opportunity for a quick conquest. While the thong had made her laugh, she knew letting her guard down with Boudreaux could lead to disaster. It wasn't the quick fling he no doubt had in mind that she objected to *per se*. She didn't consider herself a prude. She enjoyed hot, healthy sex as much as the next girl and it was a very long time since she'd had any. Plus, she had a feeling hot, healthy sex would be Boudreaux's forte. But her confidence had taken a huge hit with Andrew and she didn't want to end up feeling used again—however mutual it might be.

She'd worked out her strategy. She would be polite and distant. She must not encourage him. He was a dangerous man, both good-looking and magnetic, and he knew it. From the tone of his note, and the teasing sparkle in his eyes earlier, she suspected he would be well practised at the art of seduction. And, if that wasn't worrying enough, her attraction to him had a heat and intensity she'd never experienced before. She must not rise to the bait, or she could end up getting seriously burned.

The lift doors opened onto a plush lobby area, but Kate barely noticed it, her gaze drawn to the panoramic view of night-time Vegas on the other side of the restaurant. Past the *maître d'*'s lectern and the candlelit tables, a wall of glass showcased The Strip and the darkness of the desert beyond. Boudreaux's hotel wasn't the largest of the huge casino hotels, but it certainly had pole position. Nineteen storeys up, the neon plumage of The Bellagio, The Mirage, Caesars Palace and a host of other famous names lit up the night like a flock of narcissistic peacocks. The city, seen from this lofty angle, glowed with expectant glamour.

Kate drew in a careful breath as she approached the *maître d'* and gave him her name. She was bang on time, but as the waiter led her to a booth at the back of the restaurant she saw Boudreaux had arrived ahead of her. He stood up as she approached, his tall, imposing physique silhouetted against the flickering neon of the cityscape.

He was wearing a conservative, expertly tailored grey suit, one hand tucked into the pocket of his trousers and his white shirt unbuttoned at the neck revealing a few wisps of chest hair. Kate realised he looked relaxed and completely at home in his surroundings. Tall, dark, handsome and devastatingly sexy. As her pulse buzzed in her ears and the Morris dancers went for broke in her stomach she wondered if she had overestimated her ability to resist the irresistible.

Zack had been sitting at the table for ten minutes, nursing a Scotch and soda and debating whether the thong might have been a tactical error at this stage in the game. He'd bought it on impulse and dashed off the note because the thought of getting Kate all fired up again had amused him. But once he'd been shown to their table, he'd begun to wonder if he might have overplayed his hand.

Did the woman even have a sense of humour?

But as soon as he spotted her walking towards him through the dim lights of the restaurant, Zack found all his misgivings obliterated by an explosive surge of lust.

She looked stunning. The gold threads in her dress caught the candlelight, shimmering over her curves and accentuating the way the material clung to every delicious inch of her. She was taller than he'd first thought, her blonde hair piled up on her head with a flash of blue silk and her smooth bare legs finished off with a pair of glittery gold heels. Whether or not she had a sense of humour, she certainly had a sense of style. The outfit looked like a throwback to the days of Marilyn Monroe, but it worked on her. His eyes drifted down to her cleavage where the pale flesh of her breasts strained against the fabric. His mouth went bone dry.

Marilyn, eat your heart out.

He made a mental note to give the boutique manageress a raise for her inspired product purchasing. Kate gave him a polite smile as the waiter placed the menus on the table and excused himself.

'Hello, Mr Boudreaux,' she said in that snooty, husky voice that made him think of warm flesh and soft sheets. 'I hope I didn't keep you waiting?'

'Call me Zack.' He took the hand she offered. Her fingers trembled and he caught a whiff of the perfume she wore. Sultry but subtle, the provocative scent whispered to him as she let go of his hand. He resisted the urge to bury his face against her neck and breathe it in, but only just. 'You were worth the wait,' he said, letting his gaze wander over her figure. 'That's one hell of a dress.'

'Thank you.' She smoothed her hands over the silk and sat down, the picture of demure, but he caught the spark of mischief in her eyes as they met his. 'Better than a bathrobe, then?'

His lips quirked. So she did have a sense of humour. Damned

if he wasn't going to have fun tonight. 'Depends,' he said, 'on what you've got under it.'

Regrets, he decided, were for wimps.

With his emerald eyes hot on hers and his devastating face relaxed in a challenging grin, Kate felt all her good intentions jump up and shoot straight out of the window. 'Gosh, are we talking about your knicker fetish already?' she said in her haughtiest voice. 'I thought you'd at least let me have a drink first.'

He barked out a laugh, his eyes glittering with appreciation. 'Okay, let's get you a drink.' He snapped his fingers at the waiter. 'But I've got to warn you, this fetish is fast becoming an obsession.'

'Really, Zack?' The corner of her mouth inched up. 'That doesn't sound very healthy.'

The waiter arrived and she ordered herself a glass of Kir, conscious of Zack studying her the whole time. The trickle of awareness became a torrent.

'You're right, it's not healthy,' he said, once the waiter had gone, his voice low and intimate and full of fake concern. 'Maybe I need therapy?'

'Or maybe you should stop sending thongs to women you don't know.'

The glass of cassis-tinted wine arrived and she took a fortifying sip.

'That might work,' he said, the gravity in the words not the least bit convincing. 'Or maybe I should get to know her first.' He reached across the table, stroked his thumb across the back of her hand. 'How does that sound?' The light touch had heat spearing up her arms and across her chest.

Okay, not just practised in the art of seduction, more like world class. And to think she'd thought he was forbidding in his office earlier. He wasn't forbidding, just extremely dangerous. But the perilous urge to play with fire overwhelmed her. Why not? After the day she'd had, a bit of harmless flirtation would do her good.

'As long as you're not talking about getting to know her in the biblical sense—' she took a sip of wine, her mouth suddenly dry '—because that's going to bring us right back to your knicker problem again, isn't it?' she said, her voice tapering off as his eyes flashed hot and a muscle in his jaw tensed.

He arched one black brow, the heat in his gaze undimmed. 'It won't be a problem for long, Kate. I guarantee it.'

Uh-oh, Kate thought as the temperature in the room soared and a blush spread up her chest. This flirtation was nowhere near as harmless as she'd intended. He was looking at her as if he'd stripped her naked already. The fireball of need between her thighs meant he might as well have done. She had to cool things down now, or they'd both go up in smoke. She wasn't playing with fire here. She was playing with an inferno. And she had no idea how to handle it.

Zack knew the instant he'd gone too far. Colour stained her cheeks and her eyes clouded over. He thought it was a shame, but he didn't blame her. He'd never got so hot, so quickly before in his life. Hell, when she'd put her lips on her wine glass, his blood had gone south so fast he got a little light-headed.

She opened the menu, a slight tremor in her hands as she studied the listings in silence. She lifted her head, a nervous smile on her lips. 'Shall we order? I'm really hungry.'

He was hungry too, he thought, hungrier than he'd been in a very long time, and he wasn't thinking about food. But he nodded, picking up his own menu. 'Sounds good to me.'

He allowed her to let the conversation drift to harmless small talk as they ordered.

The quiver in her voice a moment ago had been a big red stop sign. As much as he would have liked to drive right through it and risk the crash, he knew he shouldn't. He'd found out as a young man that patience was more than a virtue. It was a pleasure. It got you what you wanted, but allowed you to savour it first.

He had a feeling that Kate Denton—with her smart mouth, her lush little body and her sassy sense of humour—would be worth savouring.

The food was exquisite, and Kate was starving, but by the time the delicate slice of chocolate pecan torte was placed in front of her she'd barely managed to swallow a bite. She couldn't seem to stop babbling. Maybe it was the intense way he absorbed everything she said. Or the questions he asked, as if he really cared what she had to say.

He knew London well, had lived there for several years in his teens, apparently, and they'd chatted about her home town for most of the meal. It should have been a relaxing, innocuous conversation, but every time she caught his eyes flicking down to her lips, every time she noticed the sexy way his mouth curved when she said something sharp or funny, her blood pressure shot up another notch.

She placed a spoonful of the rich chocolate dessert onto her tongue. It tasted dark, sensual and delicious, despite the jumble of nerves and excitement making whoopee in her tummy.

'How's your pie?' he said, his gaze dropping to her mouth again. Her pulse jumped.

'Fabulous.' She licked her lips, shocked by the reckless thrill when his eyes followed the movement. 'Chocolate should be one of the seven deadly sins, don't you think?'

'I thought it was,' he said, his voice as rich and sinful as the chocolate.

It is now, thought Kate, spooning up another mouthful of chocolate. 'Do you fancy a taste?'

'I thought you'd never ask,' he said, the intensity in his gaze convincing her they weren't talking about her dessert.

She lifted the spoon. Wrapping strong fingers round her hand, he guided it to his lips. As she watched the thick velvety chocolate being devoured the well of desire she'd been holding back geysered up. Her nipples tightened against the smooth silk of her dress and her thighs tensed, unable to hold back the flood of heat. The sensual battle she'd been waging with her body all evening had been well and truly lost.

'Thanks. That was delicious.' He caressed her fingers before releasing her hand. She saw the glow of triumph in his eyes and realised he knew he'd won.

It didn't take him long to claim the spoils.

'Kate,' he said, leaning back against the leather booth, one forearm resting casually on the table. 'You're beautiful, you intrigue me and I'm very attracted to you. I'd like to make love to you tonight. How do you feel about the idea?'

Well, he was certainly direct and to the point, she thought, her breasts throbbing now, her heartbeat pummelling.

She should have said she wasn't attracted to him, that she didn't want to make love. It was sheer madness to encourage something so reckless, so impulsive. But the lie refused to come out of her mouth. It was as if some devastating chemical reaction had taken control of her body and wouldn't let her utter the words.

Maybe it was madness, but it wasn't just that she couldn't say the words—she knew she didn't want to. Zack Boudreaux was every woman's fantasy. And the way he was looking at her right now was giving her heart palpitations. She'd never been this sexually aware of anyone before in her life. This man could make her forget the mess she was in—if only for one night. Didn't she deserve at least one fleeting chance of escape?

Kate concentrated on his face, revelling in the rush of desire as she decided on her reply. 'I feel quite enthusiastic about the idea, actually.'

His eyes widened and she wondered if she'd shocked him

with her forwardness, but then the deep green ignited with passion. He threw his napkin onto the table and stood up. 'We need to go to my penthouse, then' he said, his voice a little hoarse. Towering over her, he took her arm and hauled her out of the booth. 'Before my knicker fetish gets the better of me.'

She laughed, giddy with excitement as he wrapped his arm around her waist and steered her out of the restaurant.

CHAPTER FOUR

KATE WATCHED AS ZACK slid his passkey into the lift panel. Slipping it back into his pocket he turned to her. 'Time to get down to business,' he said.

Kate pressed against the lift wall as he walked towards her. *Okay, woman, you asked for this. Do not pass out.*

He rested one hand against the panelling above her head and leaned over her. He was so close she could see the crinkles at the corner of his eyes, the slight bump marring the perfect line of his nose. The musky scent of him filled her nostrils—a potent mix of soap, aftershave and industrial-strength pheromones.

'What business did you have in mind?' The question came out on a breathy sigh. Goodness, she'd practically melted into a puddle of lust already and he hadn't even touched her.

He cocked his head to one side, his eyes sweeping over her face. She heard the rustle of fabric as he took his other hand out of his trouser pocket. The brush of blunt fingertips on her bare leg made her quiver. 'I'm making it my business to find out what you've got on under that dress.'

She gasped as his fingers stroked under the hem of her dress, bunching the silk as they trailed upwards. 'Do you think that's wise?' she said, although she was already past caring. 'What if someone else gets in the lift?'

'This is my private elevator.' He ducked his head, nuzzled his lips against her ear. 'No one gets in here but me.' He bit into the lobe, sending a riot of chills pulsing across her nerve-endings.

She shivered violently and dropped her purse. She didn't even hear it hit the floor through the throbbing in her ears. Raising her arms, she stretched against him, pressing her breasts into the solid wall of his chest, threading her fingers through the short, silky curls at his nape. She turned her head and his lips were hot on hers. Firm and wet, his tongue thrust deep. She shuddered, tasting chocolate and man and pure, unadulterated lust.

Then his questing fingers found her bare buttock and he stilled. 'Damn!' He pulled back, his breath feathering her cheek. He stroked the naked flesh, and slipped his finger under the satin string. 'You're wearing the thong?'

'In this dress?' The words choked out on a sob. 'Of course I am. I wouldn't want a VPL.'

'A…what?' he rasped as his fingers continued to explore her intimately.

'A visible panty line.' She gasped.

His thumb traced across the core of her and he groaned. 'I'm a dead man.'

She pulled his face back to her, nibbled kisses along his jaw. 'If you die now, Zack, I'm afraid I'll have to kill you.'

He gave a gruff laugh. 'Fair enough,' he murmured, pushing her against the wall, his strong body enveloping her.

Placing hot palms on her bare backside, he lifted her. 'Put your legs round my waist,' he demanded, the teasing gone.

She did as she was told, her centre throbbing at the unyielding pressure straining against his trousers.

She clung on as he walked out of the lift. Strikingly modern, esoteric luxury surrounded her but she saw only glimpses, impressions—all her thoughts and feelings concentrated on the heat and hardness between them—until she caught their reflection in the hall mirror. She was wrapped around him like a wanton, her dress hiked up to her waist, his large hands dark against the pale skin of her bum.

She watched her skin flush red, before he strode into the bedroom. A huge bed dominated the sparsely furnished space, long drapes on the far end of the room were drawn back revealing the same romantic view of Vegas at night. His breathing was harsh against her hair, her body so hot she could barely breathe.

He let her down, slowly. The soft swish of their clothing as their bodies brushed sounded like a force ten gale. The thick wool carpet tickled Kate's bare feet. She must have lost her sandals in the lift.

Putting firm hands on her shoulder, he turned her away from him and stood behind her. She heard the sibilant hiss of her zipper and then his teeth nipped the bare skin of her shoulder. He dragged the dress off with impatient hands, then unclipped her bra. Her breasts swelled as he released them from their lacy confinement.

She looked up, pulled in a jerky breath. The sight of the two of them reflected against the night was unbearably erotic. She, naked and trembling but for the wisp of red satin underwear defining her sex. He, tall and dark and dominant behind her, still fully dressed. His hands cupped her breasts, the rough skin of his thumbs stroking across the stiff, sensitive peaks. Then he captured the nipples in his fingers, tugged. She moaned, her legs shaking as the bolt of heat rocketed down to her core.

Their eyes met in the glass.

'You're exquisite,' he murmured.

She felt exquisite, she realised, for the first time in her life.

She turned, desperate to see him, to feel him too. She pushed at his jacket, her hands clumsy in her haste.

'Hold on. I've got it.' He stepped back, shrugged off the jacket and pulled the shirt over his head, buttons popping.

Her eyes devoured his firm, muscled chest. A sprinkle of dark hair thinned over a taut mouth-watering six-pack and arrowed down to his groin. 'You're not bad yourself,' she whispered.

His trousers did nothing to hide the strength of his arousal. 'I want you inside me,' she whispered.

Good Lord, had she just said that out loud? The blush burned into her cheeks.

He wrapped one arm around her, bringing her flush against him. Strong fingers ploughed through her hair, making the swatch of blue silk flutter to the floor and her curls cascade down. 'I intend to be—and soon,' he said, before his mouth covered hers in another bone-melting kiss.

His chest hair abraded her nipples while his tongue did devilish things inside her mouth. She writhed against the storm of sensations. Trailing unsteady fingers down the smooth, firm skin of his abdomen, she cupped him at last. The heat and length of him pulsed against her palm through the fabric. He groaned and shifted away. 'Let's get into bed before I embarrass myself.'

As he stepped out of his trousers and boxer shorts her eyes devoured the magnificent erection. Her gaze lifted back to his face. 'I hope your condoms are extra large,' she said, only half joking.

He laughed, pulled her against him and tumbled them both onto the bed. 'Don't worry,' he whispered next to her ear, one powerful leg pinning her to the bed. 'I'm practically a boy scout.' His teeth tugged on the lobe. 'I'm always prepared.'

He fastened his lips on hers, his tongue insistent, tangling deliciously with hers as his hand swept down her curves, kneading her breasts, caressing her hip. He moved away for a moment to pull the thong down her legs. As his lips came back to hers insistent fingers slipped into the swollen folds at her core.

She shuddered viciously as he probed, pushing his finger into the liquid heat. His thumb circled the burning nub of her clitoris and then stroked hard. She jerked and cried out, flooding into his hand.

'That was amazing,' he said, his voice thick with urgency. 'You're amazing.' He leaned over her, fumbled in the bedside drawer and held up the foil package. 'You want to do the honours?'

She took the condom from him with trembling fingers. 'It would be my pleasure.' She rolled the latex down the length of him, his penis twitching at her touch.

The intimacy of the gesture and the feel of him, so smooth, so strong, made the heat build again. She'd never felt so aroused, so desirable or so bold before in her life.

He cupped her face in his palms, his sensual smile as devastating as the fire in his eyes. 'Thanks,' he muttered and nudged her legs apart with his knee.

'You're welcome,' she said on a shaky sigh.

His hands held her hips, angling her pelvis and forcing her thighs wider still.

The head of his penis probed gently and then in one long, slow thrust he lodged inside her. She moaned, the fullness bringing a surge of pleasure so overwhelming it was almost pain.

He began to move, the sure solid thrusts taking him even deeper.

She sobbed, gasped, unable to control the waves of ecstasy crashing over her as he touched a place inside she had never known existed.

He stopped. 'Are you okay?' he asked, his voice strained but tender, his whole body shaking with the effort to hold back.

'Yes, it's just it feels so incredible.' She choked the words out. She'd never climaxed so quickly before or with such intensity.

'You're telling me.' He groaned. 'Hang on,' he said. 'It's about to get better.'

She didn't believe that could be true, but as he began to

move in an exquisite, unstoppable rhythm she realised she was wrong. The orgasm gripped her in a fevered fist and hurled her over the edge, only to pull her up and hurl her again.

He stiffened above her and shouted out her name as the final shuddering wave seized her and flung her over into the abyss.

'Kate, are you all right?' Zack's heart stuttered as he watched her eyelids flutter open.

Thank God—he'd thought she'd passed out there for a minute. Hell, he'd almost passed out himself. He'd never felt anything so incredible. He rested his palm against the damp skin of her cheek. 'I'm sorry,' he said, brushing his thumb across the crest of her cheekbone.

He ought to be, he thought, he'd just taken her like a man possessed.

Her small hand came up and covered his. The sweet smile that curled her lips made his heart rate slow. 'What are you apologising for, you dope?'

He rested his forehead against hers. 'That was kind of fast and furious.' He lifted his head, looked down at her. He'd never taken a woman with so little sophistication before in his life, even as a teenager. It was embarrassing. 'You didn't get much in the way of foreplay.'

She pressed a fingertip against his lips, silencing him. 'Well, now, Boudreaux.' Her eyes twinkled and her smile became more than a little smug. 'I like foreplay as much as the next girl. But a guy should never have to apologise for giving a woman her first multiple orgasm.'

He laughed, relief washing over him. 'How many did you have?'

'Honestly?'

He nodded, the surge of pride surprising him.

'I lost count.' She sat up suddenly, holding the sheet to her breasts as she beamed down at him. 'Zack, I think you found my G-spot.' Her voice bubbled with excitement. 'And to think, I always thought that was an urban myth.'

'You did, huh?' He slipped a hand under the sheet, found the soft swell of her butt. 'Well, I nearly blacked out, and that's a first for me, so I guess we're even.'

'No, we're not.' She laughed. 'I'm pretty sure I *did* black out.' She pursed her lips and held her finger against them in a deliberately comical pout. 'Oh, dear, does that mean I owe you one?'

'You know what,' he said, incredulous at the renewed rush of blood to his groin. 'Seeing as you lost count, I figure you owe me more than one.' He whipped the sheet out of her hand, grabbed her wrist and hauled her out of the bed with him. 'And I know a great way to make you pay up,' he said, dragging her giggling and squirming towards the bathroom.

Forget the thrill of the chase, he thought, the thrill of the catch was going to be a whole lot better.

CHAPTER FIVE

'YOU'RE AN EARLY RISER. I guess I didn't tire you out enough last night.'

Kate's fingers slipped on the package of Pop Tarts at the sound of the deep, sleep-roughened voice. She turned slowly to see the man she'd had the wildest night of her life with leaning against the kitchen doorway, a cocky smile on his face. He'd pulled on a pair of sweatpants, but otherwise he was gloriously naked. All tanned, leanly muscled male rumpled from the bedroom, his short hair sticking up in sexy tufts.

Her mouth watered and her stomach clenched at one and the same time.

Kate was no expert in morning-after etiquette. Contrary to her wanton behaviour all through the night, she'd never slept with a guy on a first date. Until now. What exactly did you say to a man who'd brought you to unspeakable pleasure too many times to count but whom you hardly knew? She had no idea.

'It's the jet lag,' she said, brandishing the box of breakfast treats. 'I found these in your cupboard. How do you feel about coffee and a sugar rush for breakfast?'

He yawned and stretched long arms above his head, arching his back. The play of muscles across his torso drew Kate's eyes. His arms dropped to his side. The bottom dropped out of Kate's stomach.

'Those are Joey's.' He nodded at the package as he scraped his fingers through his hair bringing his hand to rest briefly on the back of his neck. 'He'll be mad if we finish them.' He walked towards her, his bare feet padding against the smooth granite tiles of the cavernous and luxuriously appointed kitchen. He smiled, a dimple appearing that Kate hadn't noticed yesterday.

The cold marble work surface pressed into the small of her back as he stopped a few inches from her. His big body radiated heat. He lifted the Pop Tarts out of her hand and leaned across her to put them down on the surface. 'Anyway,' he said, his hands resting on her hips. 'I'm sure we can do better than that.' He pulled her against him, his thumbs stroking the silk of her dress. The light caress sizzled through her, making her toes curl.

'I could cook, or we could call room service,' he murmured, dipping his head to lick the pulse point in her neck. The sizzle flared into her breasts and her nipples hardened. 'They do great maple pecan waffles, if you're in the mood for something sweet.' He wiggled his brows at her lasciviously. 'I sure am.'

She took several shallow breaths, placed her hands on his chest and eased him back, her brain engaging for the first time since she'd spotted him in the doorway. 'Who's Joey?'

Did he have a son? Goodness, he might even have a wife? She'd seen no trace of a woman's presence when she'd done a little tour of the penthouse after waking up, but, still, he could be married. It horrified her to realise she didn't know for sure.

He straightened and let her go, studying her face. 'Don't look so scared.' He rested his butt against the kitchen's central aisle, folded his arms across his chest. 'Joey's my five-year-old godson. He sleeps over sometimes when Stella and Monty, his mom and dad, need a babysitter. Who did you think he was?'

'I just wondered,' she said, looking down at her toes, faint with relief. She forced a smile. 'You don't strike me as the babysitting type.'

'There's not a lot of babysitting involved.' He smiled, the dimple winking at her again. How *had* she missed that yesterday? 'I'm a total pushover. Joey calls all the shots. Hence the Pop Tarts. If Stella knew about those we'd both be toast. She's like the sugar police.' As he spoke his face softened and his voice deepened with affection. He obviously adored the little boy and his parents.

This was a facet of him Kate never would have imagined. It made him seem almost as sweet as the Pop Tarts all of a sudden. Why the discovery should make her stomach tighten and her breathing become even more rapid she couldn't guess.

'So how about I order waffles?' He arched an eyebrow, looking more dangerous than sweet. 'We can get to the deadly sins we missed last night while we wait.'

She laughed, feeling pretty dangerous herself. 'Did we miss any?'

He stepped back to her, his enticing male scent enveloping her as he brushed a knuckle across her cheek. 'I bet I can find a few.'

'Hmm.' She considered him, holding her tongue between her teeth. 'I'd love to take that bet,' she said.

His hand dropped from her face as he grinned. He looked so delicious, it was almost indecent how much she wanted to take him up on his offer. Disappointment covered the fire in her belly like a wet blanket. 'But unfortunately, I've only got fifteen minutes before I have to meet with your housekeeping manager, Mrs Oakley.'

To think she was going to be making beds all morning when she could have been tearing up the sheets with Zack Boudreaux. She'd had her one night of bliss, and now reality was back with a vengeance.

A line formed across his brow. 'Why are you meeting Pat?'

'I think it's just a formality.' She shrugged, turned to pour herself a cup of coffee. Looking at his bare chest was only adding to her misery. 'I filled out the forms yesterday afternoon.' She put the pot down, recalling the brief phone conversation she'd had with Patricia Oakley and the reams of paperwork that had been sent to her suite.

'What forms?'

She pulled a cup out of the cabinet, placed it on the surface with a sharp click. 'I couldn't find any milk—will black do?'

'I said, what forms?'

She looked at him over her shoulder, her eyes widening at his flat tone.

She turned round. 'The employment forms, all two thousand of them.' Cradling the mug of coffee in both hands, she blew on it, inhaled the delicious coffee scent. 'Mrs Oakley's going to sort out my social security number for me. It's a good thing Andrew didn't take my American passport with him. Or I really would have been up the creek.' She took a quick sip. It might smell like coffee, but it tasted like water. She wrinkled her nose. 'No offence,' she said lightly, 'but American coffee is disgusting.'

'Why were you filling out employment forms for Pat?'

She frowned. Why was he behaving as if she were talking in a foreign language?

'Because I'm going to work here—why else?' She narrowly avoided adding a *Duh!* It didn't seem appropriate any more. The teasing mood of a moment before had disappeared.

His brows drew together in a forbidding line.

'We talked about it, yesterday in your office, remember?' Kate prompted. 'You said you were going to ring her about it.'

'Yeah, but I didn't call her.'

'I know you didn't,' Kate said, shifting uncomfortably against the hard marble.

She'd felt pretty foolish the day before when she'd mentioned his name to the housekeeping manager. He owned the hotel, for goodness' sake, of course he didn't concern himself with trifles. Still, she'd been oddly hurt when Mrs Oakley had told her she hadn't been contacted by Mr Boudreaux, especially after getting his dinner invitation.

'It's all right,' she said with a brightness she didn't quite feel. 'I sorted it out myself. Turns out two of the maids quit last week so Mrs Oakley was more than happy when I—'

'You're not working here.' He interrupted her.

'I..? Excuse me?' Had she heard him correctly? She couldn't have.

'Kate…' his voice softened a little '…I've got a strict rule against sleeping with women who work for me.'

'Oh.' The flush working its way up her neck made her feel foolish and more than a little hurt. She hadn't realised how much she'd been looking forward to continuing their fling. She blinked, determined not to let her sadness at the dismissal show. Of course he'd only been looking for a one-night deal. So had she. When had she started thinking it could be anything else?

'I understand,' she said, concentrating on a space above his shoulder. She noticed the clock on the wall behind him and saw her get-out clause. She needed to leave before she embarrassed herself any further. 'Well, it's been fun, Zack,' she said, putting her mug down on the counter. 'But I really should be going. Mrs Oakley will be waiting.' She gave him what she hoped was an unconcerned smile. 'I don't want to be late my first day on the job.'

She went to walk past him, but his fingers closed over her arm, stopping her dead.

'You're not listening to me, Kate. You're not working here.'

She gawped at him. 'Yes, I am,' she said carefully. What was he on about?

'No, you're not,' he said, the definite edge to his voice starting to worry her. 'You don't have to now.'

'Of course, I do. I need the money.'

His jaw went rigid. 'I gave you five hundred dollars. If that's not enough, say so.'

'Don't be ridiculous.' She crossed her arms over her chest, trying to hold back her own temper. 'I don't want you to give me any more money. The more I take, the more I'll have to pay back.' Why was he being deliberately dense? 'I left four of the hundreds you gave me in the living room, by the way. Mrs Oakley was nice enough to say she'd sort out a proper advance in a couple of days. When I—'

'What are you talking about?'

She stiffened. Why was he so irritated?

He twisted away, shoving his fingers through his hair and combing it into unruly furrows. Frustration snapped in the air around him before he gave a long-suffering sigh and turned back. 'You say you need money.' He said the words slowly, surely, as if he were talking to a dim-witted child. 'I gave you money. Why are you giving it back to me?'

'Because it's not *my* money,' she shot back, annoyed at having to state the obvious. 'It's yours.'

'So what? It's only five hundred bucks. I don't want it back.'

'But I thought that was the advance we'd talked about.'

'What advance?' he said, holding his palms up in exasperation before slapping them down on the sideboard.

Realisation suddenly dawned on Kate. With it came the grinding feeling of helplessness, of inadequacy, she'd fought throughout her childhood.

'Wait a minute,' she said, carefully. 'You mean you *gave* me five hundred dollars. Why would you do that?'

She'd thought the money was an advance, but if it wasn't…? The events of the previous night came reeling back to her. Without the glow of sexual excitement, the romance of the moment, what she'd done took on a whole different hue.

She pressed her thighs together, felt the lingering tenderness and was suddenly ashamed of all the times he'd been buried deep inside her.

What had he been thinking when she'd flirted with him, when she'd thrown herself at him, when she'd come apart in his arms? She covered her mouth, scared she might throw up.

'I've got to go,' she blurted out, desperate to get away.

Zack couldn't believe his eyes as the colour drained out of her face and she turned and ran out of the room. 'What the…?'

It took him a minute, but he caught up with her in the hallway, snagged her arm. 'What's wrong with you?'

She shot him a disdainful look, but he could feel her shaking. Something had really upset her, but what?

'I thought I told you yesterday,' she said, the tears hovering on her lids. 'I'm not a prostitute.'

'What? Who said you were a prostitute?'

'You don't give someone five hundred dollars for nothing.'

So that was it. They were back to the money again. Damn, the woman had more issues than a daytime chat show. 'You were in a fix. I helped you out. It's not that big a deal.'

'It is to me.' He could see by the stubborn tilt of her chin she wasn't kidding.

She tried to wrestle her arm free. He held firm. No way was she skipping out on him until they got this settled.

'Will you let go of my arm?'

He softened his grip, but kept her in place. 'Not until you tell me what the problem is.'

'It's simple. I don't accept money from men I don't know.'

'First off,' he said, pulling her closer, 'you do know me. After what we did last night you know me pretty damn well.' He felt a stab of satisfaction when she blushed a vivid red.

'Second off, the five hundred wasn't payment for sexual favours.' Now he thought about it, he was pretty damned insulted himself. 'I've never paid for sex and I never will.'

The blush intensified, but her arm relaxed. 'Okay.' Her breath gushed out and the rigid line of her shoulders softened. 'I'm sorry I accused you of that. It's just… It looked… I don't know—it looked funny.'

'It was a gift between friends.'

She nodded. 'All right, but I still can't accept it.'

Now she was just being stubborn. 'Why not?'

'Because I can't,' she said, her voice rising to match his.

Her lips puckered up into the defiant pout he'd admired the day before. He wasn't admiring it so much any more.

'Look, calm down, okay?' He ran his palm down her bare arm, struggling to soothe while his own emotions were in turmoil. He could see the hot flash of temper in her eyes, but beneath it was something else that looked suspiciously like hurt. It bothered him he might have caused it.

He tried to figure out where he'd gone wrong. How things had got messed up so fast.

Everything had been great when he'd woken up, his body still humming from one incredible night of mind-blowing sex. He'd spent the next ten minutes lying in bed, the hazy dawn sunlight streaming over him while he'd breathed in the lingering scent of Kate's perfume overlaid with the smell of freshly percolating coffee and enjoyed some inventive fantasies about what they could do for the rest of the day.

When he'd found Kate in the kitchen, clutching Joey's Pop Tarts, the soft blonde hair he now knew was natural still damp from her shower and that sexy dress stretched across her lush rear end, he'd figured it wouldn't take him long to start making his fantasies reality. The next few days had spread out before him like a smorgasbord of sexual pleasures and he'd had every intention of digging in.

Then she'd started babbling on about Pat and employment paperwork and money and everything had gone to hell in a handbasket. Well, she could forget about working here. He didn't want her working for him, he wanted her with him—in bed as well as out—for the next couple of days, but he could see he was going to have to change tactics to get what he wanted.

'Kate, this is dumb.' He forced reason and logic into his voice. 'We hit it off last night. I've got a couple of days before I have to head out to California.' He stroked his thumb across the inside of her elbow, encouraged by her shiver of response. 'We could have a lot of fun in that time.' She didn't say anything so he pressed on. Surely she could see this was the smart option. 'You can stay here as my guest and then I'll buy you a ticket home to London when I leave. How does that sound?'

Kate didn't think she'd ever been more humiliated in her whole life. This was worse than being turfed out into a hotel corridor in her underwear. She stepped away from Zack, humiliated all over again by the terrible yearning that seized her. That her body was clamouring for her to say yes to his insulting proposal only made the situation that much more unbearable.

'I pay my own way. I always have and I always will.' She tightened her arms across her breasts, willing herself to stop trembling. 'And I'm very sorry, but, as much *fun* as we had last night, I'm not prepared to be your paid plaything for the next few days.'

He cursed softly. 'That's not what I meant and you know it.'

'Mrs Oakley's offered me a job here and I'm taking it,' she continued, grateful when he made no move to touch her. 'If you don't want me working in your hotel you can have me fired, that's certainly your prerogative.' She prayed he wouldn't do that, but she wasn't about to beg. 'But you don't have to worry about sleeping with the staff, because we're not sleeping together any more. How does that sound?'

He swore again, his big body rigid, his hands fisted by his sides. The frustration was coming off him in waves but he didn't say a word.

She walked down the hallway to the elevator with as much dignity as she could muster and stabbed the call button.

'Have it your way, sweetheart,' he said, his voice brittle, before she heard the door slam shut behind her.

Her shoulders slumped in a cruel mixture of relief and regret. The lift pinged its arrival, the sound reverberating round the empty lobby like a mission bell.

As Kate stepped into the private car she spotted her gold sandals where they had fallen the evening before. The lurid memory of being wrapped around Zack, her body quivering with anticipation, made her tense as she bent to pick up the shoes.

The lone teardrop glittered as it splashed onto the golden leather.

CHAPTER SIX

'YOU'VE GOT TO BE KIDDING me.' Zack scrubbed his hands over his face, feeling weary. 'She was coming to California with me. How am I going to get another PA so soon?' And how could a day that had dawned with such promise have turned into this nightmare?

'Seems Jill didn't take too kindly to your attitude this afternoon. She said you shouted at her,' Monty said from the other side of the booth. His friendly cockney accent rubbed Zack's last nerve raw.

'I did not shout at her,' Zack said firmly, pretty sure he hadn't. He could barely remember the incident with his PA. He'd been fixated on a certain blue-eyed temptress most of the day. 'She did a half-baked job on the report I asked for on The Grange's customer profile. All I did was point it out.'

'Yeah, well, maybe next time you could point it out with a few less decibels,' Monty replied amiably, lifting the bottle of beer to his lips.

Zack watched his business manager. 'Fine.' He took a swallow of his own beer, let the chilled amber liquid ease down his throat and forced his shoulders to relax. 'Point taken.'

Jill Hawthorne's resignation wasn't worth getting worked up about. He expected one hundred and ten per cent from his staff and paid them the salaries to match. Jill hadn't been up to the job since the day he'd hired her. It was just bad timing she'd picked today to walk off in a snit. He could have done without the aggravation.

Monty straightened in his chair and leaned forward, resting his forearms on the table. 'What were you doing in the office anyhow? I thought you were taking a couple of days off before you headed out to Cally?'

That had been the original plan, thought Zack, aggravated all over again. Until a certain Kate Denton had walked out on him bright and early this morning. After that, he hadn't been in the mood to hang out in his penthouse. Every place he looked brought back memories of her lush, sexy body and the incredible things they'd been doing to each other most of the night.

'Plans change,' he said dismissively. He wasn't about to get into a blow by blow of what an idiot he'd been with Monty. He still wasn't sure how he'd let Kate get under his skin the way she had. 'I should let you get home to Stella,' he added reluctantly, mentioning Monty's wife. 'She'll give me the look next time I see her if I keep you out drinking on your first night back.'

Monty had returned to Vegas late that afternoon after a week of meetings with Harold Westchester, the owner of the hotel Zack was buying out in California. It had been Zack's idea to meet up in the loud, lively and informal surroundings of the Sports Bar. He and Monty had spent the last half an hour going over the details of the negotiations together before Monty had dropped his bombshell about Zack's PA.

'No worries,' said Monty. 'Stel understands you wanted the low-down on how things went with Westchester.'

Truth be told, the meeting could have waited till tomorrow, but Zack hadn't been in any great hurry to go back to his bed alone tonight. And Monty was always good company. They'd been best buddies ever since their early teens, when Monty had tried to pull a short con on Zack one rainy afternoon on London's Oxford Street.

'I guess we've covered everything for today,' Zack said. 'Why don't you go on home? Tell Stella I said hi,' he finished, not quite sure where the ripple of envy came from as he said it. Sure, Monty had a beautiful wife in Stella and a real little pistol of a kid in Joey, but that kind of wedded bliss had never been what Zack was looking for in life.

'I'm good for another round, yet,' Monty said, glancing at his watch. 'Look, Zack, there is one other thing I wanted to sound you out on with The Grange buyout.'

'What?' Zack asked.

'Why don't you tell Westchester who you really are?'

Zack slapped his beer bottle back on the table with more force than was strictly necessary. 'I told you before. No way.'

'We could get a better deal out of him. I'm sure of it.'

'Don't count on it.' Zack had been after The Grange for two solid years—the fact that Westchester had no knowledge about their prior connection had been paramount to the old guy agreeing to the deal in the first place, Zack was sure of it. 'Westchester and my old man didn't exactly hit it off together. I'm not risking the deal on—'

'How do you know he blames you for what JP did?' Monty butted in.

'Drop it, Mont.' Just thinking about telling Westchester made Zack feel edgy.

'Fine, I tried.' Monty threw up his hands. 'It's your choice.'

'That's right. It is. Now, do you want another beer or not?'

'Just one. Then I better shoot off.'

Zack picked up a handful of mini-pretzels from the bowl of bar snacks, glad to have at least one thing settled. He turned to signal their waitress when something caught his eye across the darkened bar. He stared in the half-light.

Another waitress was dishing out drinks to a group of guys over by the pool tables, her blonde hair shone white in the harsh neon light. He squinted, trying to focus. It couldn't be, could it?

She walked back towards the wait-station, her empty tray dangling from one hand. Her voluptuous figure looked ready to spill right out of the uniform all the female bar staff wore.

'I don't believe it,' he murmured.

He'd recognise the soft, seductive sway of those hips anywhere.

Kate was floating. At least, that was what she tried to tell herself as she pushed through the crowd of people at the bar, her head throbbing in time to the electric guitar whining from the sound system and her heels and toes burning in the shoes she'd borrowed for the evening. She'd gone past exhausted about an hour ago, entering an alternative reality where her many aches and pains were buffered by a sea of numbness—sort of.

She dumped her tray on the wait-station and shouted out her latest order to Matt, the barman. Matt waved, not even attempting to be heard above the din, and went off to fill it.

Pushing an annoying tendril of hair behind her ear, Kate swayed slightly. She gripped the bar, steadied herself, forcing her knees to lock, and took another glimpse at the clock above the bar. The stupid thing had to be broken—the hands had barely moved since the last time she looked. Still over an hour to go till her shift ended.

She groaned, the next couple of weeks spreading out before her in a never-ending kaleidoscope of spilled drinks, over-eager hands, dirty toilets and unmade beds.

Kate forced back the depression settling over her like an impenetrable fog. It could only be tiredness. So the next few weeks were going to be murder while she held down the two jobs she'd talked her way into. She'd worked this hard before. When she'd been seventeen, and newly free of her father's influence, she'd held down three jobs to keep afloat. She could do it again. All she needed was a decent night's sleep.

Thanks to the night flight two days ago, the bedroom Olympics she'd indulged in with the very creative Zack Boudreaux last night, a day spent changing sheets and cleaning toilets and the last four hours spent tottering around on heels that were two sizes too small, Kate reckoned she'd managed about four hours sleep in the last forty-eight.

She glared at the clock again, willing the hands to move faster.

Extreme fatigue was the only reason the picture of Zack and his insatiable body kept popping back into her brain. She didn't regret her decision to turn down his insulting offer one bit. She would never be any man's kept woman, no matter how gorgeous he looked or how fantastic he might be in bed. Her mother had done that and look what had happened to her.

She let go of the bar. When she stayed upright, she pulled a long fortifying breath into her lungs. Only an hour to go, then she could collapse into bed. She vowed she wouldn't so much as twitch her little finger until ten minutes before her housekeeping shift started at six tomorrow morning.

'Katie, Katie.' Marcy, Kate's fellow waitress, elbowed her way towards Kate on ice-pick heels, her chocolate-brown eyes beaming. How *did* she walk in those shoes, Kate wondered, without dislodging a kidney?

'Honey, you hit the jackpot.' Marcy slapped her tray down on the bar and snapped the gum she was chewing.

'Oh really?' Kate said, trying to muster some enthusiasm. She liked Marcy. She was so perky she made Mary Poppins look like a killjoy. But right at the moment Kate could barely string a coherent sentence together, let alone have a conversation with someone as full-on as Marcy.

'Oh, yes, really,' Marcy said, mimicking Kate's accent, her smile so bright it was practically radioactive. 'You'll never guess who's in my Number Four booth and just asked to have you serve him his next beer?'

'Who?' Kate asked, sure she didn't want to know unless the guy was Rip Van Winkle.

'Give me a minute.' Marcy winked and shouted out an order to Matt for two bottles of premium beer. She turned back to Kate, her face still beaming excitement. 'Only the big boss man.' Marcy pointed out one of the booths near the entrance. 'He's over there with Monty Robertson, his business manager.' Marcy touched Kate's arm. 'Mr Zack "Gorgeous Butt" Boudreaux, no less.'

At the mention of his name, Kate felt the headache gnawing at her temples roar into life. Then her stomach rolled over, the burn in her feet flared up and the dull ache in her back shot straight up her spine. So much for numbness.

'Honey, he's taken a real shine to you. He asked for you special.' Marcy nudged her, still talking a mile a minute, but the words barely registered on Kate.

'Here you go, babe, three margaritas.' Matt placed the drinks Kate had ordered on her tray. As Kate thanked Matt Marcy whisked the tray away.

'I'll take care of these for you.' Marcy checked the tab and hefted the tray onto her shoulder. 'You take the beers over to Boudreaux's booth when they get here.' She wiggled her eyebrows suggestively, grinned. 'This could be your lucky night, hon.'

Before Kate could form a protest, Marcy waltzed off, weaving expertly through the crowd as she balanced the tray of margaritas on one hand. Kate stared dumbly at Marcy's back, her jaw clenched so tight it was a miracle she didn't crack a tooth.

'If I get any more lucky, I might as well shoot myself,' she grumbled.

Zack was fuming, but he was keeping a lid on it.

What was she doing working tables in the Sports Bar? If she had set out to torment him she couldn't have done a better job. Just when he was trying to get her off his mind there she was, all hot and luscious in a skimpy skirt that showed her panties every time she moved and a too-tight V-neck sweater that pumped up her breasts. She might as well have been naked, the amount of flesh she was displaying to the whole bar. Watching her walk towards him and Monty, the tray of beers held high, her head down and tantalising little wisps of hair framing her cheeks, Zack had to force his eyes to stay on her face. He guessed he must be the only guy in the place who wasn't staring at her butt.

'Wow, she's built,' Monty murmured, confirming Zack's suspicions.

'Keep your eyes to yourself,' Zack snapped, 'or I'll tell Stella you've been checking out other women.'

'I wasn't checking her out,' Monty said, sounding offended. 'I was just stating the obvious. What's between you two anyway?' Monty wasn't dumb—he'd already asked the question twice since Zack had called their waitress over and asked her to send Kate back with their beers.

'Nothing,' Zack said, determined to prove himself right, even if his mouth was drying up and his muscles tensing the closer she got. The ache in his crotch didn't mean a thing either. It was just residual heat from last night. He stretched his legs out and crossed them at the ankle, making his eyes go blank as she stepped up to the booth and slid the tray onto the table.

'Hello, Kate,' he said, his voice as bland as a slice of white bread.

'Hello.' Kate gave him a brief look before concentrating on putting the bottles on the table without spilling them.

Even in a plain black T-shirt and worn jeans the aura of power pulsed around him, intimidating her. But worse than that was the wet heat that had pooled between her thighs and the parched feeling in her throat brought on by the sight of his lean, solid length relaxed against the leather bench seat.

Her eyes connected with his. She must not show any weakness. He was watching her, the handsome planes of his face defined by the light coming from behind her.

'What are you doing here?' he asked in a slow, measured voice as if he wasn't really all that interested in her reply. 'I thought you were working for Pat today?'

'I did work for Pat today. I'm working here tonight.'

A muscle in his jaw clenched. 'I see,' he said, still in that controlled, indifferent monotone. 'You know, I don't think I want you hanging around my hotel.'

Heat seared Kate's cheeks at the callous words, the assessing, dismissive once-over he gave her.

'In fact, I'm sure of it,' he said, slinging his arm casually across the back of the booth.

He looked confident and in control. Probably because he was. The rat.

Kate slung the tray under her arm. Her fingers fisted on the hard plastic. She'd like nothing better than to pick up his fancy bottle of beer right now and pour it over his head. 'You're the boss,' she said, annoyed beyond belief by the quiver in her voice. 'I'll leave.'

She turned to go, but he snagged her wrist.

'Not so fast,' he said, his fingers clamped tight. 'We need some more pretzels first.'

Kate tugged her arm loose and glared at him. She wanted to tell him where he could shove his pretzels so badly she could taste the words.

She savoured the image for a moment, then let it go. Bone-deep weariness and despair rushed up to replace it. She nodded. 'I'll go get them,' she said.

'Eh-hum.' Monty cleared his throat loudly. 'Now, are you going to tell me what the bleeding heck that was all about? Who is that girl?'

'No one.' Zack ignored his friend, still staring after Kate as she made her way back to the wait-station. Something wasn't right.

The idea had been to goad her, get her to rise to the bait and then slap her down. It was still bugging him that she'd dumped him this morning to do drudge work. But he didn't feel the satisfaction he'd expected. In fact, he felt like a jerk. Her face had been cast into shadow by the overhead light, but she'd sounded resigned, weary even. It wasn't like her to take an insult lying down. He ought to know.

'All right, why don't you pull the other one?'

Zack looked at his friend. 'What?'

'If there's nothing going on between you two, I'm Bugs Bunny. And you know carrots make me hurl.' Monty sipped his beer and skewered Zack with a look.

Zack sighed. He knew that look. It was Monty's only-dynamite-will-make-me-drop-this-now look.

'We slept together last night, okay?' Zack said at last. He took a long swig of his beer, hoping it would ease the dryness in his throat. 'Although there wasn't a whole lot of sleeping going on.' He put the bottle on the table, his throat still dry as a bone. 'Then she decides this morning she'd rather scrub johns than date me. End of story.'

Monty studied Kate's retreating figure, then turned back to Zack. 'She dumped you?' He gave an astonished chuckle. 'You've got to be joking?'

'I'm real glad you find that amusing.'

'Not amusing, mate, more like miraculous.' Monty laughed again, his eyes darting back to the bar. 'Oh, fab, she's coming back. Maybe I'll get to see her give you the kiss-off again.'

Zack jerked his gaze up, not finding Monty's teasing at all funny. As he watched Kate approach the familiar tightening in his crotch only aggravated him more.

Kate concentrated on staying upright and channelling Mahatma Gandhi as she approached Zack's table, the mini-pretzels balanced precariously on her tray. Somehow she had to get him to let her stay till the end of her shift. She hated being a pushover, but she didn't have the energy to fight and she needed her share of tonight's bar tips. If she left an hour early, she might not get them.

'Your pretzels,' she said, putting the small bowl on the table and keeping her eyes down. Maybe if he didn't mention her leaving again she could just carry on.

'Thanks,' Zack said, sounding surly. What did he have to sulk about?

She picked the empty bowl up from the table, intending to make a quick exit, when the man sitting across from him spoke. 'Don't run off, love,' he said, his broad cockney accent surprising Kate. 'It's Kate, right?'

His smile was charming and somehow cheeky at the same time. She hadn't even noticed him when she'd been at the table earlier, but then she'd been wasting her attention on Zack. She took his hand, feeling her anxiety ebb as his grin widened.

'Yes, that's right, Kate Denton,' she said.

'Lovely to meet you, Kate,' he replied chummily. 'I'm Monty Robertson.' He let go of her hand, settled back into his seat. 'Do I detect a touch of the old country in your accent?'

She nodded.

'Londoner, right?' he asked, the warmth in his soft ebony eyes putting her at her ease.

'Chelsea, actually,' she replied, feeling ludicrously grateful to be talking to one of her fellow countrymen.

'Very la-de-dah. I'm honoured,' he said, then his face fell comically. 'You're not a bloody Chelsea supporter, are you?'

Kate laughed. 'Of course I am—best team in London. You're not one of those saddos who—' The thump of a bottle hitting the table made her head whip round.

Zack was staring at them. 'I need another beer,' he said, his voice deadly calm.

Tension knotted at the base of Kate's neck. A snide retort came to the tip of her tongue, but the sudden wave of exhaustion caught her unawares. She stepped back, trying to counterbalance the wobble in her legs and stumbled.

'Hey, love, are you okay?' She could barely hear Monty's urgent question over the buzz saw in her head.

The tray clattered onto the floor. She tried to grab the table, scared of falling, but then Zack was towering over her. His fingers grasped her upper arms, holding her upright.

'What is it? What's wrong?' he asked.

She frowned, confused by the temper in his voice. What had she done now?

The familiar scent of him assailed her, she tried to pull away, but he held firm. He turned her body and the neon light from the bar shone on her face, making her squint.

He cursed. 'You look like hell.' His voice came from miles away. 'When's the last time you slept?'

She tried to lift her hands to shake him off, but someone

had tethered ten ton weights to her wrists. 'I'm fine,' she said feebly, but she couldn't seem to stop shaking.

'The hell you are,' he said, still sounding angry with her.

She wanted to argue with him. Wanted to tell him to get lost, but all that came out of her mouth was a pathetic whimper.

The world tilted and suddenly she was floating for real, her cheek rubbing the soft cotton of his T-shirt, her limbs weightless.

'Mont, tell the bar staff she's taking the rest of the night off. I'll see you tomorrow.'

She heard the words but couldn't quite process them. All she could see was the strong column of his neck, the shadow of stubble under his chin. Embarrassment washed over her as she felt his arms tense under her knees and across her back. For goodness' sake, he was carrying her. The harsh light of the casino hit her as he walked out of the bar. She wriggled, tried to lift her head away from the rock solid shelf of his shoulder blade.

'P-put me down.' Where had that stammer come from? And why was everything whirling around?

'Forget it,' he said, sounding even surlier. 'If you can't look after yourself, someone else is going to have to do it.'

Her mind tried to grasp hold of the indignation, the humiliation she should be feeling. But she couldn't shake the thought that she was in a chilling fog and the only warm, solid thing there was him. She couldn't push him away yet, or she'd be sucked into nothingness. Shivers of exhaustion raked her body.

His arms tightened around her and she heard the reassuring thud of his heartbeat. 'Relax, Kate,' he said, his voice gentle now, coaxing. 'You're okay, I've got you.'

'Don't drop me,' she pleaded, too tired to care if she sounded pathetic.

'I won't,' he said.

She softened into his strength, shut her eyes and let the fog envelop her like a warm, comforting blanket.

Zack felt Kate grow heavy in his arms. The machine-gun shots of his heartbeat finally began to slow as the deep, steady rhythm of her breathing brushed his neck. He tucked her head under his chin, adjusted her weight as he pushed the elevator call button.

He'd just lost ten years off his life.

Shock had propelled him out of the booth when she'd staggered in the bar. But as soon as he'd felt the tremors raking her body, seen the bruised smudges under her eyes, a cruel rush of guilt had replaced it. She looked shattered.

They'd got all of two hours' sleep last night and while he'd been lying in bed most of the morning, feeling put upon, she'd been working in his hotel trying to make up the money she owed. Maybe she was nuts, maybe she drove him nuts, but the woman had guts.

The elevator button pinged and she stirred. 'Shh,' he hummed as if comforting a child. She relaxed against him. She wasn't exactly light, but still she felt fragile. He tightened his hold, stepped into the elevator and nudged the button to the penthouse.

He ought to take her to her own suite, but he couldn't do it. He wanted her with him, and not just for the obvious reason. He wanted to keep an eye on her. The urge to protect her surprised him, but he didn't question it. He'd been right on the money earlier. If she couldn't look after herself, someone else would have to do it. And at the moment, whether she liked it or not, it looked as if that someone was him.

CHAPTER SEVEN

KATE STOOD IN THE DOORWAY of the palatial open-plan kitchen, cinched the tie on the silk kimono she'd found on the end of the bed and studied Zack's back. He seemed surprisingly at home standing over the gleaming steel hob, spatula in hand. The buttery perfume of cooking eggs filled the air. The smell wasn't the only thing making her mouth water. He looked tall and gorgeous as always in a pair of worn jeans and a faded sweatshirt with the sleeves torn off at the elbows.

What was it about watching macho guys cook that made a woman's head spin? The sight wasn't helping Kate's nerves one bit.

'Hi.' Her voice came out on a silly little squeak. She cleared her throat and tried again. 'Um, good morning.'

He stopped stirring, turned slowly and gave her an easy smile. 'Morning.' He nodded towards the breakfast bar and pointed at one of the stools with the spatula. 'Take a seat. Breakfast's done.'

She didn't move. 'What am I doing in your penthouse?' she said blankly, trying hard not to be charmed.

Why was he cooking her breakfast? And what exactly had happened last night? All she remembered was passing out. She'd woken up from a deep, dreamless sleep ten minutes ago to discover herself in his bed with only a few scraps of underwear on, the mid-morning sunshine peeking through the curtains on the huge picture window.

It didn't look good.

'We'll talk after we eat,' he said, dishing the eggs onto plates already loaded with bacon and toasted muffins. 'You want to grab the coffee?'

She didn't want coffee, or breakfast for that matter. Her stomach was tied in greasy knots of apprehension. The only thing she did remember was making a complete fool of herself last night—swooning like the heroine in a bad B-movie. But she had absolutely no clue as to what had happened afterwards.

Had they made love?

If they hadn't, why was he being so friendly now? He'd as good as ordered her off the premises last night in the bar.

If they had, she didn't think her pride would ever recover.

Zack transferred the plates to the breakfast bar, which he'd already laid with cutlery and glasses of orange juice. He frowned when he looked up.

She was still rooted in the doorway.

'Okay, spill it, whatever it is,' he said, sounding exasperated. 'I spent twenty minutes cooking breakfast—I don't want to eat it cold.' He placed the coffee pot and a couple of mugs next to their plates and waited.

Kate had always believed in being direct. Still she had to force the words out. 'Did we sleep together last night?'

His eyebrows shot up and then he laughed. Kate's back stiffened like a board. He slid onto one of the stools, keeping his bare feet on the floor, and poured himself a cup of coffee, still chuckling.

Heat rose in Kate's cheeks. She wrapped her arms round her waist. 'What's so funny?'

He looked at her over the cup, still grinning at the private joke. 'Sweetheart, you've given my ego some major-league hits in the last couple of days.'

The self-deprecating shake of his head and the warmth in his voice made Kate relax a little. 'How so?'

He took a gulp of his coffee, put the cup down and patted the stool beside him. 'Sit down and I'll tell you.'

She hesitated, then walked to him and lifted herself onto the stool. Propping her feet on the foot bar, she tugged the silk over her bare legs.

He put a hand on her knee. She tensed, only too aware of the warm pressure through the cool silk, and the clean, devastatingly familiar scent of him.

'All I'm saying is, when I make love to a woman, the lady usually remembers it in the morning.' He lifted his hand. 'And I don't take advantage of women when they can't say no.' He fixed his eyes on hers. 'You were out cold last night. So I took one of the other bedrooms.'

'Oh, well, that's good.' She should have been relieved, but for some inexplicable reason she wasn't, quite. 'Thanks.'

'You're welcome,' he said, picking up his fork. 'Now, eat up.'

She did as she was told, suddenly at a loss as to what to think. Okay, so they hadn't slept together, but why was he being so nice to her, then? They'd hardly been on good terms the night before.

As soon as she tasted her breakfast, Kate's appetite pushed the doubts to one side in a surge of hunger. She tucked into the light fluffy scrambled eggs, crispy bacon and hot buttered muffins, savouring every delicious bite. She was polishing off her second cup of coffee when she noticed he'd finished his breakfast and was watching her.

She put down her cup.

'I see you found the robe,' he said casually. 'It suits you,'

Kate looked down at the luxurious blue silk kimono embroidered with a flame-breathing dragon down one side. 'It's beautiful,' she murmured, pulling on the lapels. 'Whose is it?'

As soon as she'd asked the question, she wished she could

take it back. No doubt one of his other conquests had left the silk robe behind. She knew she had no claim on him, but somehow the thought of sitting in his kitchen in some other woman's clothes made her lose her appetite.

'I was given it on a business trip to Japan,' he said, refilling his coffee-cup. 'Over there, guys wear those things, too. It's not really my style, though.' His gaze wandered over her figure. 'It looks better on you.'

Kate let out the breath she'd been holding, and then felt annoyed by her reaction. Why should she care who the kimono belonged to?

She wiped her mouth with her napkin. 'Breakfast was delicious, Zack. Thanks, it was nice of you.'

'Not really,' he said, his expression unreadable. 'I owed you an apology.'

'You did?' Why did she feel as if she was missing something vitally important here? 'What for?'

'For behaving like a jerk yesterday morning and last night in the bar.'

She blinked, surprised by the admission. She had assumed apologies weren't his style any more than silk kimonos were. 'Apology accepted, then.'

Time to leave, she decided, before she let that smouldering look get the better of her again. Popping off the stool, she reached for his plate.

He took her wrist, stilled her hand. 'What are you doing?'

'I thought I'd clean up, before I go.'

'No need,' he said, turning her hand over. 'The housekeeping staff'll get it later.' He stroked his thumb across the pulse point, making her shiver. Then he lifted her hand to his lips and bit softly into the pad of flesh at the base of her thumb.

A sharp dart of desire shot straight down to Kate's core.

'Don't,' she said, curling her fingers into a fist. She tugged on her hand.

His eyes locked on hers, making her feel both trapped and needy. 'Why not?' he said, his voice gentle but firm. 'What are you afraid of, Kate?'

You, she thought, the panic making her throat constrict. It had been hard enough walking away from him yesterday morning. Kind and considerate were the last things she would have expected from him. They pulled at a place deep inside her she didn't want pulled at. There was nothing between them except one night of spectacular sex, and it would cost her if she ever forgot it.

'I have to go,' she said, struggling to ignore the jackhammer thumps of her heartbeat. 'I need to check out of my suite today, and then I have to find another job.'

He let her hand go, swore under his breath. 'Why are you so hung up on paying your way?'

'I'm not hung up on it.' She'd rather die than tell him the real reason—it was far too personal. 'It's just, it's important to me, that's all.'

'Yeah, I get that.' Frustration hardened his voice. 'I was the one who stopped you falling on your face after you'd worked yourself into a coma, remember.'

The words came out harsher than Zack had intended. When he saw her flinch he could have kicked himself. Here he was trying to persuade her to stick around and he'd blown it, already. How did the woman get him worked up quicker than a wolf at a rabbit convention? He was famous for being smooth with women, and yet with her he found it all but impossible to keep his cool.

'Yes, I do remember,' she said, her shoulders ramrod straight under the floating silk. 'I also recall you telling me to leave your hotel. Which is what I intend to do, so you won't have to pick me up off the floor again.'

'Kate,' he said, aiming for easygoing. 'I'm not having that

same argument all over again.' Okay, maybe easygoing was going to be a stretch.

'Good, because neither am I.'

She tried to walk past him. He stepped in front of her.

Defiance flashed in her eyes but behind it was something else. Something he'd seen the night before when he'd held her. Something that looked a lot like vulnerability. It gave him the cue he needed to say what he had to say.

'I've got a proposition for you.'

Her eyes flared and he had to suppress a grin.

'Not that kind of proposition.' Well, not quite anyway. 'It'll be worth your while. I swear. If you'll sit down and listen.'

She still looked mutinous.

'Please.' The word made him feel uncomfortable, but when she huffed and sat back on her stool he figured it had been worth it.

'All right, I'm listening,' she said, her chin still thrust out.

She looked stiff as a poker, perched precariously on the edge of the stool, but at least he wasn't watching her cute rear end walking out the door.

Now, how to say what he wanted to without setting her off again?

Luckily for him, he'd spent most of the night giving the problem a whole lot of thought and he had a plan. All he had to do was stick to it.

When he'd got her up to the penthouse the night before, his first concern had been getting her out of her outfit without waking her up.

It had been an exquisite kind of torture, the flowery scent she wore making him instantly hard as he'd recalled just how hot and ready she'd been in his arms the previous evening. He'd had no trouble keeping his thoughts G-rated, though, once he'd eased off her shoes and seen the raw, reddened skin on her heels and toes.

The guilt had swamped him. He'd tried to tell himself it wasn't his fault that she'd worked herself to exhaustion. He wasn't the bastard who'd stranded her in a foreign city with no clothes, no money. But he hadn't quite managed to convince himself. The feeling of responsibility and the urge to keep her safe were as strong, if not stronger, than they had been when he'd carried her out of the bar.

He'd never met a woman as independent, as self-sufficient as she was or as determined to prove it. And he'd certainly never met a woman he wanted to take care of before. That the thought was arousing as well as infuriating was just another one of the contradictions that made his reaction to this woman unique.

He'd spent the previous day sulking, telling himself she could go hang herself for all he cared. But once he'd been sitting on the edge of his bed, watching the gentle rise and fall of her breathing, he'd had to admit that whatever it was that was between them, it wasn't over. Not by a long shot.

While he'd been sitting there in the half-light considering that startling fact, a part of the conversation they'd had during their first meeting had poked at the back of his brain. Had she told him she'd been working as Andrew Rocastle's PA? The possibility had seemed almost too fortuitous to be true so he'd had the concierge pull out Rocastle's registration details and then made a late-night call to Rocastle's company offices in London where it had been already morning. He'd spoken to a very helpful personnel woman who'd pointed out that Kate Denton had indeed worked as Rocastle's PA until an 'unfortunate incident' two days ago. He knew all about the 'unfortunate incident' and it hadn't put him off in the least. Anyhow, he only need offer her a two-week contract. If she wasn't up to the job he was offering her it hardly mattered. Her typing skills weren't the main reason he wanted her at his beck and call.

Kate Denton was a fire in his blood he needed to get out.

A few weeks with her working as his PA ought to cure him of his obsession once and for all—and if she did a halfway decent job, all the better.

Having decided to give the idea a shot, the only remaining obstacle was figuring out how to make Kate go for the deal. He'd stayed up half the night working out his strategy. Cooking her breakfast had been the first part of the plan. He'd stumbled, badly, by letting his frustration show a moment ago. Now he had her back on the stool and marginally willing to listen to what he had to say, he wasn't about to make the same mistake again. Keep calm, he thought, keep cool and give the carrot the hard sell. He could get to the stick later, if he had to—he had the connections to stop her from getting any other jobs in Vegas—but for now, he figured the carrot was his best option.

'The truth is, Kate, I'm in a fix and I need your help.'

'What kind of a fix?'

'My PA quit yesterday and I need someone with me in California for the next couple of weeks. How about it?'

'You want to employ me? As your PA?' Kate was so astonished, it was a miracle she didn't fall off the stool.

'Yeah. I can only offer you a two-week contract,' he said, as if he were discussing the weather, 'but it'll be a lot more dough than you can get doing bar work and I'll cover your expenses during the trip, naturally.'

'You're not serious?' Surely this must be some kind of joke? He didn't say anything, just looked at her, his eyes steady, his lips curving ever so slightly. 'You *are* serious,' she said, completely incredulous.

'I need to close a deal I've been setting up for over two years. I'm selling my holdings in Vegas, buying a resort hotel in Big Sur called The Grange. Great coastal location, established clientele, with loads of potential for expansion and modernisation. I need someone to handle my planner, do the secretarial stuff as I hammer out the final details of the negotiation with the owner.'

'Oh, I see,' Kate murmured, her pulse scrambling into overdrive as her mind whizzed through the possibilities.

This could be the answer to all her prayers. A proper job, a challenging and exciting job that didn't involve wielding a loo brush or toting a tray of margaritas looking like a pornographic sports groupie. She might not have liked Andrew much, but she'd adored being his PA and she'd been good at it too. Just from the lowly jobs she'd done over the last day, she knew The Phoenix franchise had a much higher profile than Andrew's piddling Covent Garden design firm. Of course, it was only for two weeks, but in two weeks she could pay off her debts, get some invaluable experience to add to her CV and prove her...

Whoa, there, girl.

Kate's enthusiastic ramblings slammed to a stop as they ran full tilt into a brick wall. There was one humongous problem with the sparkling career opportunity she was being offered— and it was sitting right in front of her with a sinfully tempting smile on its face.

'So what do you say? You want to be my Girl Friday?' the devil said.

Kate gave her head a quick shake, trying to clear out the burst of stardust that had momentarily short circuited her brain cells.

The problem was, she wouldn't be working for Andrew. She'd be working for Zack. Gorgeous, irresistible, domineering Zack, who insisted on having everything his own way and would be entitled to demand it if he were her boss. As his PA she'd be working closely with him. Handling all those minute details that could feel so personal, so intimate. Hadn't Andrew once joked that Kate was so efficient she was part personal assistant and part wife? Coming from Andrew it had seemed like an innocuous compliment. If she allowed herself to get into that role with Zack she'd be in considerably more danger. Maybe she ought to clarify what it was he was expecting of her. 'Do you mind if I ask you something?'

The corners of his mouth quirked up in a knowing grin and she cursed the blush that worked its way up her neck. 'Sure, ask whatever you want,' he said.

She licked her parched lips. 'What do you expect from me, exactly?'

'What do I expect?' He rolled the question off his tongue as if he were savouring the words. 'Hmm, let me see.'

The blush scorched Kate's cheeks as she waited for his answer and she clutched the silk tighter. She wondered if the penthouse's air conditioning had suddenly gone on the fritz, because she could have sworn the temperature in the kitchen had just shot up by a good ten degrees.

'Apart from typing, shorthand, that kind of stuff, I expect you to be available twenty-four-seven. I'll be honest—I'm not always the easiest guy in the world to work for.' His gaze flicked to her cleavage. 'At times I can be real demanding.' His eyes moved back to her face, the dimple winking in his cheek. 'But then you already know that.'

Kate felt the melting sensation between her thighs and squeezed the muscles tight. How infuriating that she was unable to deny her instinctive response to him even though she knew he was being deliberately provocative.

'Stop teasing me,' she said firmly. 'It's not remotely funny.' The very last thing she wanted to do was look this gift horse in the mouth. She wanted this job, desperately, and probably not just for the career opportunity it offered if she was being completely honest with herself. But she wasn't about to serve herself up on a platter, job or no job.

He laughed easily, held up his hands in surrender. 'Okay, Kate, I'm sorry. But the look on your face. It was irresistible.'

'Answer the question. Why are you offering me this job?'

He skimmed his thumb across her cheekbone, his eyes bright with appreciation. 'We were pretty spectacular together our first night out. You're smart, you're beautiful and you're desirable and I had a hard time forgetting about what we got up to after you walked out on me yesterday morning. So I'll admit, one of the reasons I want you with me in California is so we can get up to a lot more of the same.'

It was just as she had suspected. Kate sighed. He was only offering her this job so he could jump back into bed with her. The fact that she didn't feel nearly as indignant about it as she should made her feel like a besotted fool. 'I can't accept the job under those circumstances and you know it.'

Zack leaned against the breakfast bar, but he didn't look disappointed—just the opposite, in fact. 'Hear me out here. I'd like to make love to you again. I'm not going to pretend otherwise. We were good at it. But I don't pay for sex. While we're in California, you'll be working your butt off as my PA, and while you're doing that I'll be calling the shots, because I'm the boss. But what happens in the bedroom is private and between us. It's not part of your job description. And I sure as hell don't intend for it to be a chore,' he finished, sounding exasperated.

She let out an unsteady breath. At least he'd been totally honest with her. But could she even consider such a proposal? 'What if I said I won't sleep with you?'

He shrugged. 'If you wanted to say that you could and it wouldn't affect your employment.' A sensual smile spread across his face. 'But I've gotta warn you now, I'll do my best to change your mind.'

Fabulous, Kate thought weakly, feeling the familiar inferno flare to life in her belly. What she had here was essentially a frying-pan-or-fire situation, then. Whatever way you looked at it she was liable to get burned. Because she knew she wasn't going to say no to what he was offering. Unfortunately, she had a bad feeling that the real temptation wasn't just the promise of a fulfilling day job or the night-time fun and frolics that were going to be even harder to resist. The simple pleasure of spending time with him, working side by side with him, getting to know what made him tick, was by far the most tempting possibility of all. And that was the reason why she should say no. If she let her guard down, if she allowed him to insinuate his way into her heart, she could get badly hurt.

But somehow she couldn't bring herself to do the sensible thing and say no. He was looking at her expectantly, the intensity in his face playing havoc with her pulse rate.

Surely, if she was careful, if she knew the risks going in, she could take what he offered, enjoy it and survive with her heart intact. Men did that sort of thing all the time. Why shouldn't she? Independence was the key. She had to make sure that if she compromised anything, she didn't compromise that. Then her heart would be safe. Never need anyone who doesn't need you and never sacrifice anything you can't afford to lose. Her father had taught her that lesson as a child, she had to make sure she didn't forget it.

She breathed out, her mind made up. 'I'll take the job.'

His eyes widened. She'd surprised him. Truth was she'd surprised herself more.

'Great.' He stroked her arm. 'That's fantastic. I'll get Monty to work up a contract and then we'll discuss your salary. But I guarantee you, it'll be enough to get you back to London next month in style with a nice chunk of change in your pocket.'

'Okay,' she said, the thought of going home so soon making her feel as if she were standing on the edge of a very deep precipice already.

'So we've got a deal?' he asked.

'Yes, I suppose we have.' All she had to do, really, was

make sure that, whatever happened between them, she kept a good, firm grip on reality at all times. That had always been her mother's mistake. It wasn't one she was about to repeat.

She thrust out her hand. He looked down at it, but shook his head. 'Not good enough,' he said quietly, pinning her with a gaze that scorched her skin. 'Not nearly good enough.' Threading his fingers through her hair, he tilted her face up to his, slanted his lips across hers.

The kiss was so sudden and so hot, it seared her down to her toes.

When he finally lifted his head, she felt as if she'd been branded.

'There,' he said, framing her face in large palms. 'Now we've got a deal.'

Twin tides of joy and dread swelled inside Kate as she stared at her new boss.

What had she gone and done now?

CHAPTER EIGHT

'WE'LL TAKE THE SHORTER one with the straps,' Zack announced to the overjoyed boutique manageress. 'Now let's see some of your evening wear.'

'Yes, sir, Mr Boudreaux,' the woman replied, snapping her fingers at the staff hovering around her. 'I'll get the models ready right away.'

Kate watched the woman and her minions rush off. The manageress's eyes had glazed over ten minutes ago, clocking up the dollar signs like a human cash register.

As soon as she and Zack were alone she turned on her boss, determined to make him see sense. She'd accepted his job proposal less than an hour ago and already she was starting to panic.

After taking a quick shower in his penthouse, she'd been whisked off in a limousine to one of Vegas's priciest and most exclusive designer boutiques. The merchandise here made the clothes she'd seen on Michelle's rail look like bargain-basement knock-offs.

'This is preposterous,' she whispered furiously. 'I don't need all these things. You must have spent thousands of dollars already. And there's no way that as my boss you should be responsible for buying my clothes.'

'Relax.'

He looked relaxed enough for both of them, she thought. His arm was slung casually across the back of her chair, one leg crossed with his ankle resting on his knee. How could he be so calm when he was spending a fortune?

'It's my money and I *am* the boss,' he continued. 'You need to look the part when we get to California.' His gaze drifted down her figure, taking in the T-shirt and jeans she'd bought from Michelle. 'The tomboy outfit's cute, but it's not going to cut it at The Grange.'

'But I could get the same effect for you for a lot less money. Remember how much you liked that dress I wore to dinner?'

'Yeah.' His voice deepened, making the single word sound like a caress. 'I don't think I'm ever going to forget it.'

'I got it at a thrift store for twenty dollars,' she said triumphantly, sealing her argument. Or so she thought.

He chuckled. 'They say the Lord works in mysterious ways. I guess I know what they mean now.'

'Don't be ridiculous, you don't have to—' she started, only to be silenced when he placed his forefinger on her lips.

'Quit arguing.' His lips quirked. 'This is all part of the deal, so you're going to have to stick with it, sweetheart.'

'Oh, for Pete's sake.' She slumped back in her chair, pouting. The man was completely intractable. 'I was only trying to save you some money.'

'Well, don't,' he said. 'That's not your job. Anyhow, the way I see it, it's money well spent. I'm getting a real kick out of imagining you in some of this stuff.'

'Oh, you are, are you?' Her own lips twitched. She was unable to resist his teasing any longer. He was behaving like a child in a sweet shop—and making her feel like a flipping walnut whip. Light and fluffy and completely nuts.

He grinned. 'Honey, my knicker fetish and I are gonna have a ball when they bring out the underwear.'

* * *

After making her protest, and having it comprehensively shot down, Kate gave in. Who knew she'd have so much fun doing it, though? She'd always had a passion for beautiful clothes, had spent years poring over glossy women's magazines unable to afford so much as a handkerchief. Once she'd started picking out garments, she hadn't been able to stop.

If Zack was bound and determined to buy her a whole new wardrobe, she might as well have some input, she reasoned. After all, she was the one who was going to be wearing the clothes. And she hadn't failed to notice Zack's taste leaned towards the more revealing end of the spectrum. If she left all the choices up to him she'd end up looking more like his mistress than his PA, and freezing to death to boot. It might be sweltering in Vegas in May, but she doubted it would be that hot on the Californian coast. He welcomed her suggestions, encouraging her to pick out whatever she wanted and—true to his word—didn't seem remotely bothered by how much they were spending. Consequently, Kate decided to lay the blame at his door when they got back into the limousine an hour later and she watched the boutique's doorman load box after box of their purchases into the boot.

Why had she let him buy all those clothes for her? It felt rash and indulgent. And what did it say about her precious self-sufficiency?

'What's the problem?' Zack watched Kate's teeth tug on her bottom lip as she gazed out of the limo's back window. She looked dazed.

He'd had a whale of a time buying the clothes—and not just because he wanted to see her in them. Watching the way she enthused over fabrics and designs, checked the texture of every item, marvelled over the stitching and the craftsmanship, had reminded him of the passionate way she made love—with nothing held back. It was a shame she couldn't be like that all the time.

Seeing her let go of the hang-up she had about money, if only for a little while, had made him wonder about it. Someone must have hurt her deeply once, for her to be so cautious, so careful about her independence—and he was certain it went a lot deeper than that loser Rocastle.

She collapsed back into the seat, gave him a concerned smile. 'I'm wondering how I can justify spending so much when I'm only going to be working for you for two weeks.'

'Simple,' he said, enjoying her confusion. He'd bet she'd never treated herself before in her life. 'You don't justify it. I spent the money, not you.'

She frowned. 'Actually, that makes me feel even worse.'

'You're going to look a million dollars in your new clothes. The money's not a big deal. Get over it.' He lifted her hand to his lips, buzzed a quick kiss across her knuckles. 'Now, how about we head back to the penthouse and have a nice long lunch?'

She sat upright, eased her hand out of his grasp. 'But I thought we were going to be working this afternoon. I need to start familiarising myself with everything. Aren't we leaving for California the day after tomorrow?'

'That can wait,' he said, knowing his indifference was going to bother her more. Somehow, teasing her was becoming addictive. He loved watching her blue eyes darken to a vivid turquoise and those plump, kissable lips get even more pouty. And anyway, work was the very last thing on his mind at the moment. 'There's a few other things I'd like to familiarise myself with first.' He pressed the driver's intercom button, resisting the chuckle as her forehead puckered up. 'Take us back to The Phoenix, Henry,' he said.

Zack clicked off the button, settled back in the seat. 'As I recall, we've got some unfinished business, you and I.' He toyed with one of the curls that had escaped Kate's pony-tail, loving the soft, silky texture of it. He was already anticipating the feel of it draped over his chest.

Panic closed Kate's throat. She could see from the possessive look in his eye exactly what he had in store for this afternoon and lunch didn't have anything to do with it.

She swallowed heavily. As much as she craved the thrill of what they could get up to in the privacy of his penthouse, she had to start setting some boundaries. For herself as well as for him. The limo, the designer clothes, the casual, proprietary way he looked at her, touched her, had already thrown her off balance.

If they leapt straight back into bed, it would only make that harder. She had to establish herself professionally, start showing him what she was capable of as his PA before she became anything else. Maybe it was pride, but she wanted him to see that he hadn't made a mistake hiring her, even if he had done it for all the wrong reasons.

He tucked the tendril of hair he'd twirled round his finger behind her ear. 'If something's bothering you, why don't you spit it out?' he said indulgently, putting his hand on her knee.

Her back went up even more. That confidence of his really did need to be taken down a notch. Another good reason not to go straight back to the penthouse and do just what he wanted, however hard it was going to be to say no.

She bit into her bottom lip, trying to find the right way to tell him. 'In the words of the great Mick Jagger,' Kate began, grasping for something approaching gravity, '"you can't always get what you want".' She lifted his hand off her leg, shifted away from him. 'And in some cases it's better if you don't.'

He laughed. 'Mick sure as hell never said that last part.'

'That's not the point,' Kate continued, determined not to be sidetracked. 'You hired me to do a job. I want to get a chance to do it before we... I mean, if we decide to...' She sputtered to a stop. Great—she sounded like a complete ninny now.

He was grinning at her, as if he found her incredibly amusing. 'If we decide to what?' he asked, raising an eyebrow. He placed his hand on her waist, stroked warm fingers under the hem of her T-shirt. 'If we decide to do this, you mean.'

Kate shuddered at the contact. She grabbed his hand, pulled it out. 'I'm trying to have a sensible discussion here,' she snapped.

'Your idea of a sensible discussion is misquoting Stones lyrics?' he asked.

Right, that wasn't a smile on his face any more. It was a smirk. She wasn't putting up with it any longer. 'I'm being serious.'

'Are you playing hard to get?' He leaned closer. 'Because I've got to tell you, it's turning me on.'

She put her hands against his shirtfront, pushed him back. 'I'm saying I don't want to make love with you this afternoon.' The words were shaky but distinct. She could see he had got the message when he frowned.

He sat back; his glance flicked down to her nipples. 'That's not what your body's saying,' he remarked calmly. Reaching up, he touched one rigid peak through the cotton of her T-shirt. She gasped as the spear of need shot straight down to her toes.

He dropped his hand, having made his point. Blast. He was still smirking.

'Why don't we cut to the chase?' he said. 'We both know you want me as much as I want you. We're two healthy, consenting adults who happen to be great in bed together. There's no reason why we shouldn't mix business and pleasure over the next few weeks.'

She took a deep breath, tried to steel herself to be as honest as she could. 'It's just…' She hesitated. 'I don't think jumping back into bed with you is a good idea.'

'I disagree.' He tugged on one of her curls again. 'I think it's a great idea.' He watched the tendril as it sprang back before looking at her face. 'Why don't you?' he asked so bluntly, she flushed.

She forced herself to ignore the fluttering in her stomach at the determination in his gaze. 'You said yourself you have a strict rule against sleeping with women who work for you.'

'Rules are made to be broken,' he countered.

'You'll be my boss—sleeping with you will complicate our working relationship.'

'No, it won't,' he said without a moment's pause.

Could he really not see the problem at all?

She was at a complete loss about what to say next when the chauffeur swung open the door to the limo and tipped his hat at Kate. 'We're here, ma'am.'

She stepped onto the pavement, heard the door slam behind her as Zack got out on the other side. He walked round the car to join her. 'I say we go up to the penthouse and discuss this further,' he said as he put a possessive hand on her back and led her towards the hotel's entrance. She obviously hadn't got through to him at all, she realised.

She stopped and turned, dislodging his hand. 'I'm not going to the penthouse with you.' There, she'd said it. Now all she had to do was stick to it.

His eyebrow lifted. 'You sure?'

From the self-assured look on his face, it occurred to her she absolutely had to win this round if she was going to maintain any kind of control on this relationship at all. She might be deluding herself about being able to resist him for two whole weeks. But she needed to prove to him she wasn't a pushover. He liked to dominate. She had to show him that he couldn't dominate her. 'Yes, I'm positive,' she said as firmly as she could manage.

He pushed a fist into the pocket of his trouser. 'All right. We'll leave this discussion for another time.'

'And until we go to California,' she announced hastily, 'I'd like a separate room, please.' That got another raised eyebrow, but nothing more. If he was annoyed, he was hiding it well.

'I guess that can be arranged,' he said, calmly.

'Thank you,' Kate murmured, feeling oddly dispirited. But as she went to walk into The Phoenix ahead of Zack she snagged her wrist and pulled her back. He leant over her, the whisper of his breath against her ear making the sensitive skin of her neck tingle.

'You can have it your way for now.' He pushed her hand behind her back, trapping her against him. 'I can wait,' he murmured, his lips inches from hers. 'I'm very good at waiting, until the cards fall the way I want them.' There was no mistaking the sensual threat before he pressed hot, firm lips to hers.

Her lips parted and his tongue thrust into her mouth, devouring her as her body moulded to his. Just as she felt herself losing control, the heat scorching her insides, he stepped back. He held her steady as her breath gushed out. Taking her hand in his, he pressed his lips to her hair, whispered against her ear. 'But I won't wait for ever.'

The kiss had been quick, fleeting even, but also devastating. Kate trembled as she walked across the lobby to the reception desk, unbearably aware of the man beside her.

Good Lord, she'd just been branded. Again!

CHAPTER NINE

'HE WANTS TO PAY ME four thousand dollars for two weeks' work! But that's completely ridiculous.' Kate gaped at the contract Monty had given her to sign.

Zack's business manager chuckled. 'I told you, he's a generous employer. Don't worry—knowing Zack you'll be working your socks off for it.'

Which was exactly the problem, Kate thought, slapping the pen down and thrusting the contract back across the desk. 'I can't sign it. That's far too much money.'

Monty looked at her for a moment, then grinned. 'You know, it's funny, but he said you'd say that.'

'He did?'

Was that why she hadn't seen him since their little disagreement yesterday morning? She dismissed the notion. Don't be daft. One thing Zack had never been was afraid of a confrontation with her.

The cold weight settled more firmly in Kate's stomach. There could only be one explanation for his vanishing act over the last day and a half. He'd lost interest in having anything other than a business relationship with her. Which was great, she tried to assure herself, even though she knew her pitiful behaviour that morning told a different story.

She'd been sent a curt note by one of Zack's secretaries

telling her to report to his offices. Assuming he'd be there, she'd spent a good half an hour picking out an outfit from her new wardrobe and preening in front of the mirror.

When she'd arrived in a silk wraparound skirt and blouse ensemble by Nicole Farhi only to find Zack gone for the day, she'd been miserably disappointed. It had taken a titanic effort to write notes on The Grange deal instead of second-guessing herself over the decision to make him wait. She shouldn't give a hoot that she'd blown it with him.

Then she'd been ushered into Monty's office and presented with Zack's ludicrously generous contract. And now she was all over the place again. What exactly did Zack think he was paying for? And why didn't she feel as indignant about it as she should?

Monty pulled open his desk drawer and lifted out a piece of folder notepaper. 'He told me to give you this if you put up a fight.'

Kate unfolded the heavy paper. Written in Zack's distinctive black scrawl were just three sentences. Kate read them, felt a surge of excitement and blushed scarlet.

> Stop getting your proper knickers in a twist.
> I don't pay for sex.
> Z
> PS: Especially if I'm not getting any!

A bubble of laughter burst out without warning. She slapped her hand over her mouth to hold it back and it came out as a snort.

'You okay, love?'

She eased her hand down, her face hot enough to fry an egg on as she took in Monty's concerned frown. Good grief, had Monty read the note? He probably thought she was a complete tart. She gave what she hoped was a ladylike cough. 'Yes, I'm fine, thank you for asking.'

'Ready to sign the contract yet?' he asked amiably.

'Of course,' she said, holding on to her composure. She took the contract, signed it with a flourish and pushed it back across the desk—the picture of cool, calm professionalism.

'Great,' Monty said, checking her signature and then standing up to offer Kate his hand. 'Good to have another Londoner on board.'

She grasped his fingers, mollified somewhat by the genuine warmth in his eyes. Maybe he didn't think she was a total slut.

As Monty led her out of the office and started introducing her to 'the team' Kate made herself a solemn promise. She would be the best PA Zack Boudreaux had ever had. She would work so hard over the next two weeks, Zack and everyone else at The Phoenix would be blown away by her efficiency, her industriousness and her unimpeachable work ethic. She was going to earn every single solitary cent of those four thousand dollars—so that no one could imply she'd got this job by sleeping with the boss.

'You know, you look really familiar. Are you sure we haven't met?' Kelly Green asked, sending Kate an inquisitive half-smile as she handed her yet another file on The Grange deal.

'I've been staying in the hotel—maybe you've seen me about,' Kate said, concentrating on the file to hide her guilty blush.

She'd recognised Kelly instantly. The plump, pretty secretary had been sitting outside Zack's office gaping when Kate had been marched up there in her underwear and a bathrobe. Luckily Kelly hadn't been able to place her. Yet. 'I must have one of those faces,' she continued, the insincere smile making her cheeks ache.

'Oh, well.' Kelly shrugged. 'I can already tell you're a lot nicer than Jill.'

'Who's Jill?'

'Mr Boudreaux's last PA. The one in the hot seat before you,' Kelly replied in a sing-song voice, obviously keen to chat.

'Do you know why she left?' Kate asked, more curious than she wanted to admit.

'Sure, she quit a couple of days ago after Mr Boudreaux blew up at her. But I think he would have kicked her out pretty soon anyway. Jill was a whiner—and he doesn't put up with those for long, let me tell you.'

That didn't sound too encouraging. Was Zack the sex god also Zack the slave-driver? In Kate's position, that might not be a good combination. 'He doesn't sound very sympathetic.'

'He can be hard on you if you don't get the job done right,' Kelly said, carefully. 'And he's famous for being ruthless in business. There's even rumours he used to be a professional poker player before he built The Phoenix,' she added, as if she were divulging a state secret. 'But he's never shouted at me before,' she finished, sounding almost disappointed.

'So Jill wasn't any good?' Kate asked hopefully. Her mission to dazzle would be easier if she wasn't replacing someone with a pristine reputation.

'That—and she was always coming on to Mr Boudreaux in the office.'

Kate blinked. Fabulous. So the man already had a history of sleeping with his PAs. Why was she not surprised? 'They had a relationship?' she asked dully.

Kelly looked round, making a quick check on the two other secretaries who were handling some filing on the other side of the office. She perched herself next to Kate's chair and said in a conspiratorial whisper, 'Jill always made out like they did to me. She went on and on about the trip to California, even booked them into the same cottage at the resort. Course, she knew we were all pea-green with envy.' Kelly sighed. 'He's such a hottie, who wouldn't want to spend two weeks alone with him in a hotel?'

Who indeed? Kate thought huffily. So much for Zack's strict rule about sleeping with his employees. It was lowering to realise she wasn't the first of his underlings to be charmed out of her knickers.

'But you know what?' Kelly continued, standing up. 'I think Jill was full of you-know-what. I never once saw him respond to any of her flirting. If anything it seemed to annoy him. I think she quit because she'd finally figured out he was never gonna be interested in her.'

Or she'd discovered Zack was replacing her with a newer model. The man was obviously a serial seducer of his staff.

'I see,' Kate said, giving Kelly a sympathetic nod and trying not to feel hurt. What had she expected? He'd talked her into bed in less than a day. And she could hardly pretend she hadn't enjoyed every minute of it. 'Thanks for telling me all this. It's always good to know the lay of the land on a new job.'

'No problem,' said Kelly. 'My advice would be, do your job the best you can and don't flirt with Mr Boudreaux. But then I can tell you're a lot classier than Jill. That must be why he hired you.'

Not quite, thought Kate, feeling more compromised than ever as she watched Kelly walk back to her own desk. She opened the file Kelly had handed her, but the words and figures blurred as she considered her position and exactly how impulsive she'd been up to now.

She hadn't exactly been very classy either, but she was going to do her best to be classy from here on in. Which meant no more recreational sex with the boss whenever he clicked his fingers. She was not about to become another notch on his bedpost.

Kelly was right about one thing. Until Kate knew how to handle Zack, and her overpowering attraction to him, there could be no more flirting.

CHAPTER TEN

'MONTY SAYS YOU SPENT yesterday getting up to speed on The Grange deal,' Zack said, unfastening his seat belt.

'That's right,' Kate replied. She smoothed her skirt down, noticed the way his eyes followed the movement. She cleared her throat, ignoring the dancing butterflies in her stomach. Surely the weightless feeling was only because Zack's private jet had just reached its cruising altitude.

Luckily, Zack had been all business since meeting her at the airport, which was handy, because her resolve not to flirt with him had already taken a few hard knocks. He looked tall, dark and delicious freshly showered and shaved and wearing a navy-blue perfectly tailored Hugo Boss suit and white shirt. Her heart had been beating double time ever since they'd entered the jet, the subtle scent of his aftershave making the luxury tan leather interior unbearably intimate. She hadn't bargained on being alone with him so soon, but he'd dismissed the cabin attendant right after take off.

What she needed to do now was keep the conversation as businesslike as possible or she'd be totally sunk. Heated looks like the one he'd just flicked down her legs would be ignored at all costs.

She pulled the report she'd been working on the previous evening out of her carry-on bag. 'I've typed up my notes on the history of the negotiations,' she said in her most forthright, no-nonsense voice. 'Monty said it would be useful for you to have it all in writing. All the aspects you've already agreed with Westchester and anything that's still to be decided before the signing.'

His eyebrow lifted but he took the file. She jerked when his fingers touched hers on the document and prayed he hadn't noticed her reaction.

'You've been busy,' he said at last, leafing through the pages. 'This looks very thorough.'

'That's what you're paying me for, remember,' she said tartly, and instantly regretted it.

His lips curved. 'So you got my note?'

'Yes, I got your note,' she replied, flustered. This was the last thing she should be talking about. 'I thought it was completely inappropriate,' she said, aiming for outrage and getting breathless instead.

He dumped her report on the coffee-table and, crossing one leg over the other, tapped his open palm on his ankle. 'As I recall,' he said, 'appropriate behaviour isn't your strong suit.'

'It is now,' she said, trying to convince herself.

'There's no need to change your ways on my account,' he said, a devilish glint in his eyes. 'I'm a big fan of your inappropriate behaviour.'

'I don't have time for that any more,' she said recklessly, layering as much simpering subservience into her voice as she could muster. 'I'll be too busy working.'

He flashed her a laser-sharp grin. 'Well, hell, Kate. I thought a good PA knew how to multitask.'

'I'm superb at multitasking,' she said, determined to ignore the innuendo. 'My shorthand and typing are exemplary, as are my communication skills.' Businesslike and abrupt ought to shut him up.

He gave her a deliberate once-over. 'As you know, I'm more interested in your other skills.' A shiver of awareness shot up Kate's spine.

The man had no shame. Why wasn't she outraged?

'Yes, but you're not paying me for those, remember?'

'I know I'm not.' He reached across the table and brushed a knuckle across her cheekbone. 'I was thinking more in the region of a free trade.'

The soft touch and suggestive comment had images of their one night together blasting into Kate's mind.

'I don't think so,' she said. Could he sense the fireball of need searing her insides? She saw the challenging grin and decided retreat was her only option.

Fumbling with her seat belt, she leapt up and walked to the aeroplane's window with as much poise as she could manage. Staring at the candyfloss clouds, she tried to even out her breathing. Well, her attempt at classy and businesslike hadn't exactly been a roaring success.

'Look at me, Kate.'

She turned to find him standing close. Too close.

'Why are you sulking?' he asked, amused and indulgent.

And so much for her grand plan to put him in his place. 'I'm not.'

'Sure you are.' He slid his finger under her chin, lifting her face, then stroked his thumb across her lower lip. 'The pout's sexy as hell, you know.'

'I'm not pouting, either,' she said, pulling away. 'This is me looking annoyed.'

'Yeah?' He curled his fingers round her nape. Her sex throbbed hot as he got closer still. 'Then I guess I better annoy you some more,' he murmured against her lips.

The smart thing to do would have been to push him away. Her mind registered the thought, but then his mouth covered hers, his tongue pressing against her lips, demanding entry—

and smart crashed and burned. She let him in on a sigh, her fingers clutching at his shirt.

Why did he have to be such a fantastic kisser?

He dragged her against him. The blatant evidence of his arousal, hard against her belly, had her sanity returning. She wanted his respect, and she wasn't going to get it if she melted the instant he crooked his finger. The realisation brought the thought of Jill Hawthorne and all his other conquests to mind. She let go, pushed him back.

He dropped his arms. 'Still sulking?' he asked mildly, his breathing only slightly uneven. Did the man never lose his cool?

'I have no intention of becoming one of the herd.'

His brow furrowed. 'What herd?'

'How about we start with Jill Hawthorne?'

'What about Jill Hawthorne?' He looked genuinely stumped.

'You know, your previous partner in multitasking,' she announced, getting a good firm grip on her indignation at last.

'My…?' His eyebrows shot up and then, to her astonishment, he laughed.

'It's good to know you find it funny,' she snapped. At least he could have the decency to be ashamed of his track record. 'I bet Jill didn't.'

'That's so cute.' He took her arms, still chuckling as he rubbed his palms up the thin silk. 'You're jealous.'

'I most certainly am not jealous,' she said, trying to shove the green-eyed monster back down his hole.

'Yeah, you are,' he said. 'And I think I like it.' He paused for one last chuckle. 'But I've got to tell you it's misplaced. Jill and I never multitasked.'

'You didn't?' She would not be glad.

'I told you already. I don't sleep with my staff.'

'But what about me?'

'You're the exception to my rule. The one and only exception so far.'

'Really?' She would not feel special either.

'Yeah, really.' He took her hand and led her back to her seat. 'But you're right about one thing.'

'I am?'

He waited for her to sit down and then sat in his own seat. 'We should have talked about this before, but I got distracted.' He gave her a sheepish grin. 'I always do with you.'

And she absolutely, definitely would not be charmed.

'Talk about what?' Kate asked, trying and failing to stifle the warmth spreading up her torso from the gruff intimacy in his voice.

'Our sexual histories. This is the twenty-first century and it's the smart thing to do.'

'Oh,' Kate exclaimed, not sure what to say. This conversation threatened to be even more dangerous than the last one. And look where that had got her.

'To put your mind at rest,' he carried on, in the same supremely confident tone, 'I always use condoms and I'm not quite as prolific as you think. The last woman I dated was over three months ago and we only lasted one night.' He gave her a crooked smile. 'She was nowhere near as distracting as you.'

'Oh, well, that's good,' Kate said, a blush spreading up her neck again. For goodness' sake, she was not a blusher, but she'd done more blushing in the last few days than the whole rest of her life put together.

He rested his forearm on his knee. 'So, what about you and Rocastle? Were you sleeping together?' The question sounded casual. A bit too casual.

'No, we certainly were not.'

'Good.' He sat back, looking pleased. 'Any guy who treats a woman like he did—whether she's his employee or not—is a jerk.'

'I know,' she said, grateful for his support, even though it seemed a bit misplaced. 'But to be fair to Andrew, he didn't put nearly as much effort into seducing me as you are.'

'His loss,' he said, apparently not taking the hint. 'So how long had it been for you?'

Kate's blush intensified. She was not about to tell him her last sexual relationship before him had been well over two years ago. He'd gloat. And it would put her at even more of a disadvantage. 'I don't want to answer that question,' she said, delicately.

'That long, huh?' he said, gloating.

Drat, was he a mind reader now, too? 'Could we please stop talking about this?'

'Sure,' he said, sounding even more self-satisfied. He picked up her report from the coffee-table. 'Why don't you call the flight attendant and organise our lunch while I read this?'

And just like that, they were boss and PA again. Kate should have been overjoyed, but she wasn't. The abrupt turn-around provided more proof, if proof were needed, that he was the one in charge. He set the agenda for their relationship and she didn't seem to be able to do a thing about it.

She opened her mouth to speak, to protest his high-handed attitude, when he reached into his jacket pocket, pulled out a pair of horn-rimmed spectacles and put them on.

He glanced up at her sharp intake of breath. 'What is it?'

'You… You wear glasses?'

She'd never been particularly attracted to guys in spectacles before. But, good grief, those piercing green eyes were even more devastating in the slightly nerdy frames. They made him look vulnerable. Which was an illusion, of course, but a very sexy illusion nonetheless.

'I'm near-sighted,' he said matter-of-factly. 'I don't wear my contacts on the plane because of the dry air.'

'I see.' She recrossed her legs, tugged her skirt down over her knees.

Get a grip, woman. Stop picturing yourself ripping his clothes off and ravishing him in nothing but his glasses right this instant.

She stabbed the intercom button and arranged their refreshments with the flight attendant while Zack bent his head to study her report.

What had happened to her carefully laid plans for getting this situation back under control? It was more out of control now than ever. Thank goodness he hadn't spotted her ludicrous reaction to his specs. It would be like a red rag to an already very confident bull.

As Zack studied Kate's impressively comprehensive report he couldn't resist a wry smile. So the glasses got her hot. Good to know. Just as it was good to know she hadn't slept with Rocastle—or anyone else for quite a while. He wasn't usually a possessive guy, but with Kate it was different.

He'd done the right thing offering her the PA's job. And, as tough as it had been yesterday to stay away from her, it had been a smart move to give her some space too. He didn't want to scare her off. He wasn't usually a pushy guy, but Kate's artless sensuality had got to him. Hell, he'd needed a little space himself.

He flicked a page over, smiled some more. After that kiss, it was clear she wasn't nearly as afraid of him as she was of herself and her reaction to him. All he needed to do was stoke that fire every chance he got and she'd come to him.

Having to wait didn't bother him one bit. Hell, anticipation was nine-tenths of the fun—and Kate's quick wit and sassy mouth would make the victory all the sweeter.

For the first time ever he could appreciate the old saying that it wasn't the winning that counted, it was playing the game. Then again, he could afford to appreciate it, because no way was he going to lose.

CHAPTER ELEVEN

THE WIND WHIPPED at Kate's cheeks as the rocky splendour of Big Sur rushed past. Unfortunately, the elemental beauty of the California coastline wasn't the only thing taking her breath away.

The roar of the convertible's engine dulled and Kate watched Zack downshift to take another hairpin bend. As the glory and spectacle of America's legendary Highway One flashed past, the spring sunshine glinted off the Ferrari's glossy red paintwork and seemed to spotlight the man beside her. Even though he'd finally taken off those sexy specs, all her senses seemed to be heightened, her awareness of him humming through her veins like a potent narcotic.

She studied his profile, the slight cleft in his chin, the hint of a five o'clock shadow on high slashing cheekbones, the Armani sunglasses that didn't quite hide the tiny laughter lines around his eyes. She battled back the heady sexual thrill that had paralysed her on the plane and took a deep fortifying breath of the fresh sea breeze.

As the car rounded another treacherous bend the dense chaparral bushes on their right gave way to a meadow of lupines, poppies and wild lilacs, blanketing the forbidding cliffs in cheerful blue and purple blossoms. Her heart slowed. What a glorious sight.

Kate closed her eyes, turned her face into the wind and tried to force herself to think sensibly. Okay, this was easily the most romantic place she'd ever been and with the sexiest man she'd ever met. She shoved her hair back, held it behind her head and took another long, calming breath of the salty air. She had to stop herself from being completely and utterly swept off her feet.

She'd known from the start how skilled Zack was in the art of seduction. What she hadn't realised was how single-minded he could be and how used he was to getting his own way. It seemed nothing could put a dent in that self-confidence. And if his towering ego wasn't already a big enough mountain to climb, the fact that she was so over-whelmingly attracted to him meant she was trying to scale Mount Everest with one hand tied behind her back.

As the coast road wound around the cliffs like an asphalt ribbon Kate peeked over the edge. It was a long drop to the secluded coves softening the ancient rocks below. But the truth was the whisper of nerves thrilled her as much as they terrified her.

Make that two hands tied behind her back.

The pressure of Zack's hand on her thigh made her pulse scramble. He squeezed her leg, shot her a quick grin. 'Awesome isn't it?' he shouted above the powerful hum of the Ferrari's engine and the rushing wind.

'Absolutely.' And the view wasn't the only awesome thing on offer. 'How far is it to The Grange?'

'About ten miles.' He rubbed her thigh. 'Wait till you see it. The location's to die for.' He put his hand back on the gear stick. 'Sit back and relax, not long now.'

Kate settled into the car's bucket seat and let the sun warm her cheeks—but she knew she'd need knockout drops before she'd be able to relax.

* * *

'Welcome to The Grange.' Harold Westchester's sherry-brown eyes glinted with appreciation as he gave Kate's hand a dignified peck.

The elderly owner of The Grange straightened and shook Zack's hand. 'It's good to meet you in the flesh at last, Boudreaux. I was starting to think you were going to let Robertson close the deal without ever seeing the place.'

Kate caught the mild note of censure in Westchester's tone. The old guy was clearly miffed Zack had never visited before. The news surprised Kate. The files on The Grange deal showed Zack had been angling to buy the place for over two years. Given his reputation for thoroughness, it seemed odd he had never come to inspect the investment in person.

Maybe that was why he seemed a little agitated. As soon as they'd taken the turn-off leading to the resort, he'd been silent and tense. He'd even stalled the car when they'd parked at the entrance to the hotel lobby.

Westchester had been waiting for them, directing an army of bellboys to handle their luggage. Kate had instantly warmed to the older man. He reminded her of her Grandad Pete, her mother's father. A wily old fella who would tell it to you straight and always had a ready hug. The fact Westchester didn't seem the least bit overawed by Zack's status endeared him to her even more. Nice to know one other person who wasn't prepared to drop to their knees and start genuflecting as soon as Zack appeared. She might have found an ally.

'I thought you were coming with Robertson during his visit last week?' Westchester continued, still sounding starchy.

Zack stiffened almost imperceptibly. 'I was tied up.' The denial sounded defensive to Kate, which wasn't like Zack at all.

'Well, at least you're here now, young fella.'

Kate had to control the giggle at the old guy's irascible tone. No, he definitely was not in awe of Zack.

'I guess we better get you and your pretty assistant checked in,' Westchester said, winking at Kate.

After signalling his bellboys, he led Kate and Zack into the hotel's wood panelled lobby. A huge central fireplace accented the high vaulted ceilings, making the place look both spacious and homely at the same time. It was neat and clean and the profusion of wild spring blooms spilling out of the wall-hangings gave it a fresh, cozy ambience. It was beautiful in a sweet, uncomplicated way, but so unlike the sleek exclusivity of Zack's Vegas hotel Kate wondered what had made him so determined to buy the place and relocate here.

Westchester introduced them to the reception staff using their first names. Kate wondered if the informality was another little dig intended to cut Zack down to size. If it was, Zack didn't seem to notice.

'Now, then,' Westchester began. 'The Ms Hawthorne who made the reservations said you'd need a two-bed cottage because you'd probably be working late together. So I stuck you in Terra Del Mar. It's got a shared bath, but it is real pretty. Hope that's okay?'

The blood surged back into Kate's cheeks. Mount Everest just got bigger. How on earth was she going to resist Zack's advances if they were sharing a cottage—and a bathroom?

'That's great,' Zack said, stroking a hand across Kate's back. In a lower voice, he added, 'I expect we'll be having a lot of late nights.'

If Westchester heard the innuendo he didn't let on. 'That's settled, then. How about we get some tall drinks in my quarters while your luggage is taken to your cottage?'

Kate was about to accept when Zack interrupted her. 'Kate's tired from the trip. We'll take a rain check on the drinks.'

'All right,' said Westchester evenly.

'Don't be silly.' Ignoring Zack, Kate put a hand on

Westchester's arm. 'I'd love to have drinks. I'm not the least bit tired.' And she had no intention of being alone with Zack again so soon. She needed more time to marshal her defences.

'I'm glad to hear it, young lady.' Westchester tucked her arm under his, patted her hand. 'I make a mean martini if I do say so myself.' But as the older man turned to make the last of the arrangements with his receptionist Zack mouthed the word 'chicken' at her.

She blinked at him. Who, me? she mimed back.

He shot her a provocative smile and raised his eyebrows. Her blood pressure soared. Oh, dear.

'I do hope you like martinis,' Westchester said as he escorted Kate down the corridor to his private quarters.

'I adore them,' Kate replied, having never tasted a martini in her life.

Despite all her efforts to keep the drinks with Westchester going as long as possible, Kate found herself alone with Zack in the Terra Del Mar suite less than an hour later.

Just as Kate had suspected, the place was a romantic dream. Zack couldn't have picked a better love-nest if he'd arranged it deliberately.

While Zack tipped the bellboys, she inspected the deluxe two-bedroom bungalow. Westchester had called it a 'cottage', but she thought the term a little quaint. A large sitting room with an open fireplace led onto a cliff-top terrace. Glancing into the master bedroom, she spotted a huge four-poster bed Sleeping Beauty would have been proud of. The image of her and Zack entwined on the coverlet came to mind and had her slamming the door shut.

'You want the double or the single?'

She whipped round at the sound of Zack's voice. He looked relaxed and amused with his butt propped against the back of an armchair. He'd taken off his jacket and slung it over the chair—and was studying her with an intensity that made her wonder if he'd just read her mind, again.

'I...' She stopped, cleared her throat. 'I'll take the single, thank you.'

He began rolling up the sleeves of his shirt, displaying tanned, muscled forearms sprinkled with dark hair. Kate's mouth dried up.

'You sure?' he asked, crossing his arms. 'Maybe we should conserve energy and share the double?'

'That's more likely to generate energy than conserve it,' she shot back.

He laughed. 'You've got that right.'

Her face wasn't the only thing starting to heat up and she suspected he knew it from the way he was watching her. Tearing her eyes away, she walked past him onto the terrace.

'Wow, this view is incredible,' she exclaimed, maybe a bit too loudly as she walked across the redwood deck.

Although she was far too aware of the man behind her, she wasn't wrong about the stunning natural beauty before her. Leaning on the rail, she gazed out over the rocky promontory. The ocean swirled below them, the waves crashing onto a sandy cove accessed by a steep wooden staircase anchored into the cliff. Secluded and spectacular, the cottage seemed to cast almost as potent a spell as the man. Spotting the bubbling hot tub at the end of the terrace, Kate deliberately turned away from it and let the brisk breeze cool her cheeks. Okay, probably best not to go there yet either.

The soft thud of his footsteps on the wooden boards seemed louder than the crash of the ocean below her. Warm hands smoothed over her belly and pulled her back against a solid chest. Zack's breath whispered against her ear as his arms hugged her midriff. 'You can't run away for ever, you know.'

She shuddered as his thumbs traced her hip bones. Her breath hitched. She fought back the swell of pleasure, turned in his arms. Seeing him so close, the deep green of his eyes, the harsh demand on his face, smelling that tantalising scent of soap and man and sexual intimacy, she realised he was right. But letting him know it was another thing entirely. After allowing him to get the upper hand on the plane so easily, she had a lot of catching up to do.

'I'm not running away. I'm standing my ground,' she said tartly. 'It just so happens I don't like to be pushed. And up till now you've been a bit pushy, Boudreaux.'

Passion flared hot and intense in his eyes as he pulled her hard against him. 'See that's where you're wrong. I'm not being pushy. I'm being honest.' He sank his fingers into her hair, scraped it back from her face. 'Unlike you.'

Fisting his fingers in the wayward curls, he captured her lips in a raw hungry kiss. Her mouth opened involuntarily and his tongue swept inside her mouth as every single nerve-ending in her body stood to attention.

Her breath panted out, the flames burning so strong, so fierce, she knew she would soon be overwhelmed. Her hands gripped his shoulders, felt the hard, unyielding muscle, the tensile strength beneath the smooth linen of his shirt, and held him back as she tore her lips away.

So much for fighting fire with fire—all she'd done was set off an inferno.

'I want you,' he murmured, his hand stroking her backside. 'Let's stop playing games.'

'I'm not the one playing games. You are.'

He stared at her. 'How do you figure that?' His breathing was a little harsh, his voice huskier than before. The knowledge gave her a much needed burst of power.

Maybe she couldn't throw his confidence, his arrogance, his conviction that he would soon have her again back in his face. After all, her erect nipples were practically boring a hole in his chest, her sex was so swollen and ready for him she had to clamp her thighs tight to stop her knees from giving way. And the heady masculine scent of him was making her head spin. But she could at least get things back on an even footing.

'I'm not prepared to jump every time you click your fingers, Zack. I want some ground rules.'

'What rules?' he asked, incredulous, his eyes skimming down her figure. He didn't sound quite so calm and in control any more. It was music to Kate's ears.

'Rule Number One,' she announced, easing his arms down. 'Just because Zack is the boss in the boardroom, does not mean he's the boss in the bedroom.'

He let her go. 'You ought to know by now, I don't play by anyone's rules but my own.' He cursed softly and raked his fingers through his hair. 'But I guess I can give you some more time to figure that out.'

She wanted to argue with him, to take offence at his dictatorial manner, his cast-iron confidence, but not a single word would come out of her mouth. Because she knew, if he'd pressed the point, they'd already be breaking all the rules. And her body wouldn't be putting up an argument.

He left her standing at the rail and marched back into the cottage. He turned in the doorway and her eyes took in the impressive bulge in his trousers. 'You've got a little while, Kate, to get used to the idea. But after that I intend to have you again. And by then, you won't want to stop me.'

She stood dumbstruck as he walked off to the smaller bedroom, snagging his suitcase on the way. Now why did the audacious statement sound more like a promise than a threat?

CHAPTER TWELVE

'TAKE OUT THE second clause here,' Zack said, pointing at the document over Kate's shoulder. 'And rephrase the third paragraph according to the attorney's instructions.' The cotton of his shirt sleeve brushed against her cheek. 'When that's done, I'll take another look.'

'Yes, boss,' Kate murmured without thinking, all too aware of the sudden drop in temperature as he straightened away from her.

'And no cheeky remarks,' he said, walking around the terrace table to sit in the chair opposite Kate's.

'No, boss,' she said, a flirtatious smile lifting her lips.

He pulled his glasses down, eyed her over the top of the horn-rimmed frames. 'Watch it,' he said, his voice lowered in warning. 'I might think you want to play.'

She bit back the provocative reply that wanted to burst out and ducked her head to start typing in earnest.

She had to stop goading him. But how could she when he was driving her insane?

Maybe it was the sleepless night she'd had, unable to get comfortable on the huge, empty four-poster bed, or the fact that he'd been ordering her about for the last twenty-four hours.

Problem was, every time he gave her another order, the promise he'd made yesterday afternoon kept running through her head. That he didn't have the slightest qualm about touching her, leaning over her, and generally getting into her personal space every chance he got, wasn't helping much either.

Much more frustrating, though, was the fact that he seemed a lot better at playing this waiting game than she was. He hadn't talked once about their personal relationship since yesterday's ultimatum. Last night he'd wished her a pleasant evening and walked off to his bedroom alone without a backward glance.

When they'd gone to dinner earlier in the evening at the hotel's restaurant, he'd watched intently as she'd licked lobster butter off her fingers, but had kept the conversation on his plans for moving his business to California. By the end of the evening, Kate had been hyperventilating. Finding six packets of condoms neatly stacked in the bathroom cabinet this morning had made things even worse. She hadn't been able to stop thinking about them and him—and what he intended to do with them—all day long. And to top it all off, he kept wearing those damn glasses. All he had to do now was take them out of their case and twirl them in his fingers and she got aroused. It was mortifying.

The only thing keeping her from giving in to the sexual tension crackling in the air was pride. She didn't want to lose this game of cat and mouse—with Zack in the role of tomcat and her in the role of obedient mouse.

He was toying with her, waiting for her to show a weakness and then he would pounce—and she didn't want to be pounced on. Well, not quite yet anyway—not until he showed a weakness too. But she was beginning to think he didn't have any. And the strain of holding back was making her crazy. Why else would she have this reckless urge to flirt with him again?

She clicked the laptop's keys, forced herself to concentrate on the job at hand and ignore the liquid pull in her belly. At least she'd managed to keep abreast of all the work he'd set her as his PA. She'd typed so hard her fingers ached, made so many phone calls she was worried she might be going deaf in one ear, and had started reciting Zack's business diary in her sleep. The job was challenging and exciting and she knew she'd impressed him with her efficiency. And he couldn't possibly know how much sexual energy she was channelling into her job to keep from leaping into his lap.

Zack watched Kate's fingers fly across her keyboard and admired the titanic effort she was making to get back on task. Good to know he wasn't the only one performing at the top of their game thanks to a raging case of sexual frustration. His groin had ached like a sore tooth the night before when they'd got back from their meal. He'd spent most of the evening staring at her lips all shiny with melted butter. He'd taken his second cold shower of the day as soon as he'd wished her goodnight, only to step out of the cubicle and be assaulted by the smell of Kate's rose-petal perfume. Had she sprayed it round the bathroom to drive him nuts? But still he'd stuck to his guns and resisted the urge to march straight into her bedroom.

She was damn well going to come to him this time.

He'd made his feelings clear. He knew she wanted him as much as he wanted her. As soon as she admitted it, they could stop kidding around. He hadn't liked her accusation that he was being too pushy with her. He was never pushy with women. They could either take what he had to offer, or leave it. It was always their choice. With her the lines had gotten a little blurred. All right, maybe more than a little blurred. As soon as she came on to him the way he knew she wanted to, they'd be crystal-clear again. He tore his eyes away from her rattling away on the keyboard and looked out over the terrace rail.

The glorious spring weather and the comforting smell of

pine resin and sea salt he remembered from his childhood lifted his spirits some more. It was good to be back. And despite the havoc Kate was causing to his libido, she'd also been lively company, a worthy adversary and a dynamo at work. He'd never had a better PA. All of which amounted to a great distraction when he needed it.

He'd expected the jolt when he saw Harold Westchester again, but he hadn't quite bargained on having all those emotions he'd spent years burying deep being wrenched back to the surface. The games he'd been playing with Kate had done a great job of taking his mind off the ghosts of his past.

He started to scroll through the emails on his laptop while letting the feeling of anticipation wash over him. The last few days of torture were going to be worth it in the long run. In fact, now might be a good time to turn up the heat on Kate. After that flirtatious little smile a moment ago, he figured she was real close to throwing in her hand.

'It's finished,' Kate said. 'Do you want to take a look at it before I print it out?'

'Sure,' he said, levering himself out of his chair. He braced his hands on the desk on either side of her, his cheek almost touching her hair. God, she smelled good.

'This looks great,' he said, scanning the copy and savouring the spurt of satisfaction when she tensed. Nope, it wouldn't be long now before she folded. 'I can't see Hal putting up any more resistance,' he said, inhaling the scent of her hair and thinking the deal with Westchester wasn't the only thing about to get settled.

'Who's Hal?' she asked, turning to face him.

'Hal Westchester, the old guy whose hotel we're buying,' he said absently. She was close enough for him to see the beguiling rim of purple round her irises.

'I thought his name was Harold.'

'Hal's his nickname. That's what I called him when—' He stopped, clamped his mouth shut. What the hell was wrong with him? He'd nearly blurted out something he hadn't spoken about in more than twenty years.

What had he been about to say? Kate had never seen him flustered before, but he'd paled beneath his tan. He pushed away from her, straightened. 'Why don't you email the—?'

'I didn't know you and Harold Westchester knew each other,' she interrupted, intrigued. What had put that haunted look in his eyes?

'It was a long time ago.' His face went hard and expressionless.

She swivelled in her chair. 'Why did you both pretend you'd never met?'

His shoulders tensed. 'Hal wasn't pretending.' His eyes flicked away. 'He doesn't remember me.'

Apprehension churned in Kate's gut. What was really going on here? Why couldn't he look at her? Was that guilt she'd heard in his voice? Did he have some ulterior motive for buying Westchester's resort? Kelly had said he was ruthless in business. But how ruthless?

'Why didn't you tell him you've met before?' she asked.

It occurred to her in that moment that, although she'd spent one unforgettable night of passion with this man—developing a major sexual obsession for him in the process—and had travelled all the way to California with him, she knew next to nothing about him. Because she hadn't asked. It was about time she stopped letting her hormones make all her decisions for her.

He turned back, studied her face. 'Stop looking at me as if I just drowned a kitten,' he said impatiently.

'Well, stop avoiding the question, then,' she replied.

His eyes narrowed and he sank his hands into his pockets. 'I don't have to explain myself to you.'

The curt statement hurt in a way Kate would never have expected. 'I know that, but we have been lovers and...' she hesitated, took a deep breath, knowing what she was about to say would end the game for good '...and we're going to be lovers again.'

The flare of arousal turned his eyes a dark jade-green. Taking his hand from his pocket, he brushed a finger down her cheek. 'Good to know you've finally accepted the inevitable.'

She pulled away from his touch. 'What's your history with Harold Westchester?'

He shoved his hand back into his pocket. 'The connection between Hal and me is old news. It hasn't got a damn thing to do with us.'

Kate acknowledged the hit. 'Of course it does. I'm not about to jump into bed with a guy who might be doing something unethical.'

'Unethical!' he shouted, genuinely outraged. 'What the hell are you talking about? There's nothing unethical about this deal. Westchester's getting a good price for the resort, more than a good price. I would never cheat him, he means—'

He stopped abruptly, turned away. He gripped the terrace rail, his knuckles whitening. She wasn't sure what she'd unearthed, but this was the first time she'd ever seen him lose that implacable cool. She wasn't about to let it drop now.

He'd collected himself when he turned back. Crossing his legs at the ankle, he leant against the rail. She could see he was trying for casual indifference. 'Look, Kate,' he said. 'It's no big deal.'

'If it's no big deal, why are you scared to talk about it?'

He shot upright, casual biting the dust in a big way. 'I'm not scared, damn it.'

'Then tell me.'

'All right. Fine.' He threw up his hands, frustration pumping off him. 'When I was eight years old, my old man checked us in here, then split. He didn't show up again for six months. That's it.'

Kate didn't know what she had been expecting, but whatever she'd been expecting it wasn't the anger that blindsided her. 'Are you saying your father abandoned you here?'

'No, not exactly.' He gave a harsh laugh. 'Jean-Pierre wasn't a bad guy. He just wasn't cut out to be anyone's father. He was a gambler. When he was on a roll, he forgot about everything else. It's no big secret. Now can we drop it?'

Not on your life, thought Kate. She'd caught a glimpse of the man behind that super-confident mask. It both stunned and fascinated her. 'Where was your mother?' she asked quietly.

He sat down opposite her, sighed. 'Do we have to talk about this?'

'Yes, we do.' More than he could possibly know.

He shrugged and looked out at the dusky light. The evening was closing in, scarlet clouds bleeding into the blue of the ocean on the horizon. The shadows on his face weren't just from the dying day, Kate realised.

'My mother died when I was a baby. I don't remember her.' He looked back at her. 'It was me and my old man and it worked fine, most of the time.'

'*Most* of the time?' she said, hating the feckless reprobate. 'Did he forget about you more than once, then?'

'Never for more than a couple of days.' He shrugged. 'Until we landed here.'

'But that's appalling.' How vulnerable and alone he must have been. A little boy abandoned by the one person who should have been looking after him. Was that why he fought so hard for control now, because he'd once had so little of it as a child?

'JP signed us in under false names, then did his vanishing act. After he'd been gone five days, I panicked.'

'What did you do?'

He gave her a crooked half-smile. 'I tried to steal some money from the motel register. Hal caught me and figured out the truth.' He sighed. 'I freaked out, swore at him, kicked him in the shins, tried to run away. I was a real brat.'

'You were frightened,' Kate said gently.

'Maybe,' he said casually, as if his feelings hadn't been important. 'I thought they'd turn me over to the cops. But they didn't. They took me in.' Astonishment tinged his voice. 'Hal's sitting room still looks exactly the same as it did back then.'

No wonder he'd been so tense when they'd walked into Harold Westchester's parlour.

'What happened when your father returned?'

He leaned his forehead on his open palm, ran his hand down his face. It seemed this memory was the hardest. 'It wasn't pretty,' was all he said.

'You should tell Hal who you are.'

He stiffened. 'No.'

'Why not?'

'Because I don't want to,' he said with a vehemence that shocked her. 'I'm not that miserable brat any more. I left him behind years ago.'

She wanted to ask him why he hated that desperate child so much. From the closed look on his face, though, she knew he wouldn't answer the question. She decided to approach the problem from a different angle. 'Why did you want to buy The Grange so much, then?'

'Honestly? I don't have a clue. I decided a while back to sell up in Vegas. But I don't know why I chose this place.' He pushed his chair back, got up. 'It was just some dumb impulse I couldn't stop.' He paced over to the rail, leaned against it, his body stiff with tension. 'When Monty started the negotiations, I got him to check out what Hal knew. I didn't want Hal connecting me with that kid.'

'I can't believe Hal would forget you so easily.'

'Hal and Mary never knew my real name.'

'You mean you never told them, all the time you were living with them?'

'No, I never did.' He paused, as if debating whether to tell her more. Was this where the guilt had come from? 'They thought my name was Billy Jensen. At first I didn't tell them my real name because I thought it'd be safer, but then...' He sighed. 'I don't know. It was like I'd become a different person.'

'You were a scared little boy,' Kate said gently. 'Believe me, Hal's not going to hold it against you if he's the man you described to me.'

'How can you know that?' His voice broke on the words, and she realised that inside the tough, commanding man there was still a tiny part of that abandoned child—who didn't think he was worth the trouble to love.

She crossed to him, laid her hands against his chest, felt the hard pulse of his heart. Her own heart squeezed in response. 'You have to tell him who you are,' she whispered. 'You have to tell him the real reason you're buying The Grange.'

'What do you mean, the real reason?'

'You want a home,' she said simply. 'And this is the only one you've ever had.'

Zack was dumbfounded. It was as if she'd reached into his soul and pulled something out he didn't even know was there. A secret yearning he'd never once admitted to anyone, not even himself. He turned away from her, stared out to sea, the conflicting feelings of guilt and remorse and longing making his stomach pitch like the surf below.

Her hand rested on his back, smoothed over his spine. 'Hal's the real reason you came back.'

He bent his head, his fingers clenching on the warm solid wooden railing. The earth had just shifted beneath his feet. It made him feel exposed and needy, the way he'd felt as a kid. The way he'd sworn he'd never feel again.

He swung round and her hand fell away. 'You're wrong. I don't need a home and I don't need Hal Westchester.'

And I don't need you either, he thought desperately. He couldn't. She'd made him feel things, think about things he didn't want to think about. It was way past time he stopped messing about and took what he did want. Her body.

He pushed back the panic, reached for her. 'How about I order us some supper?' He slid his hand down her arm. 'This sunset's too pretty to waste on work.'

The deliberately seductive rumble of Zack's voice rippled across Kate's senses. The brush of his fingertips made her skin tingle.

What she'd said had shaken him, and he was trying to hide it by changing the subject. She didn't understand why, but that glimpse of vulnerability made her want him now more than ever. The depth of her attraction still frightened her, but she was finally willing to admit that it excited her more.

'Dinner would be lovely,' she said, hurling caution to the wind. What had it done for her anyway except leave her on a knife-edge of unfulfilled passion? 'I'm famished.'

She welcomed the swift kick of lust as she watched him walk into the cottage to order room service. Her imagination ran hot as she tidied away the laptops, stacked their work papers on top.

Zack had won another hand, but they'd both be reaping the reward.

CHAPTER THIRTEEN

'I'M STUFFED,' Kate said, dropping her fork onto her plate.

'You finished already?' Zack said, glancing at her mound of uneaten pasta. His eyes fixed on her lips. 'I thought you were starving?'

Kate didn't miss the deliberate innuendo.

It was a miracle she'd been able to eat anything at all with Zack watching her like a hawk all through supper. Knowing what was in store for tonight was playing havoc with her appetite—for food, anyway.

She picked up her glass of Pinot Noir, took a hasty gulp and searched for an innocuous topic to calm her nerves. Now they were so close, she was getting jumpy.

'Is it true you were a professional poker player before you built The Phoenix?'

'You sound surprised,' he said, taking a leisurely sip of his own wine.

'I am a bit,' she admitted. 'You don't seem the type to risk everything to luck.'

'If you stay focussed and play the cards right, luck can be tamed.'

He said it with such confidence, she was honour-bound to contradict him. 'I don't believe that. If you're not dealt the cards it wouldn't matter how you played them. You'd still lose.'

'How about we have a game of five-card draw and I'll prove you wrong?'

'I don't think so.' Did she look stupid? 'I haven't got any money—and I'm not even sure I know the rules, so I'd be at a huge disadvantage.'

'We don't have to play for money.' He ran his fingertip down the stem of his wineglass. 'And I can tell you the rules.' When she didn't reply he arched one tantalising eyebrow. 'Unless you're chicken?'

'Of course I'm not,' she said, loudly. She wished he would stop caressing his glass like that. 'But what else can we play for?'

A sinfully sexy smile spread across his face. 'Items of clothing.'

She blinked. 'You're not seriously suggesting we play strip poker?'

'I've waited close to a week to get you naked again,' he said. 'I'm getting desperate.'

But he didn't look desperate, he looked like a tom-cat with a bucket full of cream in his sights.

Kate's cheeks pinked and her pulse began to race. But she couldn't get the picture of Zack naked and at her mercy with that cocksure grin wiped off his face out of her head. Surely, this was too good an opportunity to miss.

But did she dare?

She leaned round the table and assessed the situation. He had on chinos, a shirt, a belt and some Magli loafers, no socks. Assuming he also had a pair of boxers that was still only six pieces of clothing. She did a quick mental calculation of her own wardrobe. Including her earrings—counted individually, of course—and five bracelets, it made a grand total of twelve items. 'And we count everything—including jewellery?' she asked.

He laughed, his gaze flicking to her wrists. 'Sure, we can even count buttons if you want.'

Kate glanced at her cotton print dress which had about twenty-five tiny pearl buttons from the neckline to the hem and the cardigan she'd put on to chase away the night chill. Another six buttons there. His shirt couldn't have more than ten and the top two were already undone. He really was full of himself.

'That sounds fair,' she said, already savouring the thought that his confidence was going to be his undoing—literally.

'All right, then.' He stood, dumped his napkin on the table and picked up the bottle of Pinot and their wineglasses. 'So we've got a game?'

'Absolutely,' Kate said as he held her chair for her.

He steered her into the cottage's living room. After lighting the small fire in the fireplace, he went to get a deck of cards. Kate perched on the couch and studied the fire. He hadn't turned on the main light switch, leaving the licks of flame to light the room with an amber glow. Added to the luxurious silk-weave rug on the floor, the half-full bottle of rich red wine on the coffee-table, and the night perfume of jasmine and lavender drifting in from the terrace, Kate didn't think he could have set the scene for seduction more perfectly.

The flicker of arousal that had been taunting her for days flared up as he walked back into the room. He toed off his shoes and sat cross-legged on the rug, the fire highlighting the harsh line of his jaw. She stared at the bare foot peeking out from beneath his folded knee. Did he realise he'd just given her another two item advantage?

He fanned out the cards, flipped out the jokers, then shuffled with a dexterity that suggested years and years of practice. As she watched his long dark fingers handle the cards with consummate skill, Kate felt the bottom drop out of her stomach.

Why did she get the feeling she'd just been hustled by a pro?

He looked up, his gaze penetrating, and beckoned her with his finger. 'Sit on the rug, it'll be easier to deal.'

She sat facing him, tucking her legs under her butt and trying to ignore the tickle of silk under her calves and the heavy thud of her heartbeat.

Why did she feel as if she were stark naked already?

He dealt them five cards each, face down, then poured them both another glass of wine while he explained the rules. As Kate picked her cards up she didn't feel like a mouse about to be pounced by a tom-cat any more, she felt like a mouse at the mercy of a big, bad, poker-playing wolf.

'But I've got two aces!' Kate cried. He could not have beaten her again. So far she'd lost both her shoes, all her jewellery and her cardigan—and her dress was being held together with one hand while she played with the other. He'd only had to undo four measly shirt buttons.

'And real pretty they are too,' he said as his eyes swept over the gaping neckline of her dress. She scrambled to cover the pink lace of her bra. His gaze moved back to her face. 'But two aces don't beat two pair.'

'But they're only twos and threes. That's ridiculous,' she argued. She couldn't lose her dress. She'd be down to her bra and knickers.

He chuckled, scooping up their discarded cards. 'By my count you've got three items left,' he said smoothly. He looked at her, his gaze piercing enough to make the thin cotton of the dress even more redundant than it was already. 'You want me to help you out of the dress?'

'No, thanks,' she remarked tartly, covering the hitch in her breath with bravado.

The way things were going, she might as well have offered to do a striptease for him. The fact that she felt unbearably turned on only made the situation worse. Her plan these last few days had been to make him realise he couldn't always be the boss. But he was more in charge now than ever, and she'd handed over control like a lamb leading its own way to the slaughterhouse.

What made it all the more mortifying, though, was the fact that he had stayed focussed just as he'd said he would, while she'd been distracted by every single hot look he'd sent in her direction.

The brush of his fingers on her leg made her jump.

And he still had that cocky grin in place.

He stroked his open palm over her knee. 'You're not a welcher, are you?'

She shivered. 'Of course not,' she said, pride warring with nerves as she got up on shaky legs. His gaze took its own sweet time working its way up her figure. Everywhere his eyes touched burned as she edged the dress off her shoulders, held it close and then let it go. It dropped to the rug, billowing around her feet. His jaw hardened and his eyes flashed with green fire before he looked down to shuffle the cards.

She stared at the waves of dark hair on his head, his shoulders broad beneath the white linen. From this angle she could see the ridged muscles of his abdomen through the opening in his shirt.

Hang on a minute. Why wasn't he looking at her? And why hadn't he said anything?

Her nipples peaked against her bra and goose-bumps pebbled across her flesh despite the warmth of the fire. Could he really be so unaffected when she was about to explode?

But then she noticed a muscle clench in his cheek and the small adjustment he made to his trousers as he shifted his sitting position.

Maybe he wasn't quite as comfortable—or as focussed—as he wanted her to believe.

She silently cursed her own stupidity. What was wrong with her? She'd been an easy mark. She should be using all this bare flesh to her advantage instead of behaving like a shrinking violet. She sucked in a breath. It was about time she gave him a run for his money.

Kicking the dress to one side, she knelt on the rug. Placing one hand flat, she braced her arm against her chest, pumping her breasts up until they were practically bursting out of the pink lace. She cleared her throat. Zack glanced up and his eyes widened. The muscles of his jaw tightened even more. Well, he was certainly looking at her now.

'Why don't I deal?' she said, doing her best imitation of Marilyn Monroe.

He raised an eyebrow but then his gaze strayed back down to her cleavage. He coughed. 'No problem,' he said, his voice strained as he handed her the deck.

She ran her nails across the back of his hand as she took them, felt the ripple of reaction. That was more like it. Poking out the tip of her tongue, she slid it across her upper lip while she dealt the cards. She could have sworn she heard a muffled groan.

As he reached forward to collect his cards she shot a quick look below his belt.

The rush of feminine power made her feel more confident than she had in days. Just as she had suspected, her opponent wasn't nearly as focussed as he was pretending to be and she had some very impressive evidence to prove it.

Her luck was about to change.

She fanned her cards and spotted two queens.

Skill and focus be damned. He was going to lose his shirt—and a lot more besides.

Kate watched Zack frown at his cards and couldn't resist a grin. Another bum hand for Mr Poker Man. After she had tried every seductive trick she could think of in the last twenty minutes his game had gone to pieces.

Pretending to study her own more than adequate pair of

tens, she slipped her fingertip under the lacy edge of her bra and ran it down the plump swell of her breast with a lazy sigh.

He swore under his breath.

'Pair of twos says you take the bra off, now,' he snapped, throwing the pitiful hand face up onto the rug.

'Well, what do you know?' Kate waved her cards in his face, savouring her moment of triumph. 'It appears my pair of tens wins.' All he had left on were his Calvin Klein boxer shorts. She pointed at the obscenely stretched cotton, her own sex throbbing with anticipation. 'Hand over the Calvins, buster.'

'Not till I get the bra.'

'Sorry, no can do.' She flapped her tens at him again. 'I won.'

To her utter shock, he clamped strong fingers round her wrist, whipped the cards out of her hand and flung them into the fire. 'Game's over, sweetheart.'

'You can't do that!' she shouted, staring at her winning cards as their edges curled up in the flames.

'Wanna bet?' he said, standing up and hauling her with him.

In one smooth move, he trapped her arms behind her back, manacled them in one hand, and covered her gaping mouth with his.

She struggled, panting, consumed by fire as his tongue thrust into her mouth and she was crushed against the broad, unyielding chest she'd been ogling a minute ago. He tasted of wine and frustration. Hunger seized her and she pressed into him, her mouth accepting the dominance of his tongue, her belly melting against the hard ridge in his boxer shorts.

The sharp snap hurled her back to reality. She tugged her arms free, mortified to see her breasts spilling out of the bra cups. He pushed the lace straps off her shoulders as she grabbed for the bra. The struggle lasted less than a second before he whipped it away and flung it over his shoulder.

'Give that back,' she cried, clasping her arms over heaving breasts.

'You cheated,' he announced. 'You pay the price.'

'I did not cheat,' she said, outraged as she scrambled back.

'Deliberate distraction and provocation counts as cheating.' He stalked towards her.

'It does not. You made that up.' She slapped her palm against his chest to ward him off. But then the backs of her knees hit the sofa and she collapsed onto it.

He pounced, pinning her arms down and pushing her into the cushions with the weight of his body. 'Now for your punishment,' he murmured, dipping his head. His rough tongue lathed across one swollen nipple.

She shuddered, moaned as he captured the peak and suckled hard. All her righteous indignation was incinerated in a firestorm of lust. He transferred to the other breast, stroking the underside before tugging the turgid flesh with his teeth. She choked out a sob, need soaking her knickers.

His weight disappeared suddenly and she opened her eyes. Yanking her upright, he lifted her effortlessly over his shoulder.

'What are you doing?' she demanded in a daze, her hands braced against the firm muscles of his back as he carried her into the bathroom.

She could hear him opening the bathroom cabinet. The packets of condoms she'd spotted earlier that day flashed into her mind. 'Getting supplies,' he said. 'It's going to be a long night.'

She barely had a chance to register that shocking announcement before he'd marched her through into the bedroom and dropped her onto the four-poster bed. Two boxes bounced next to her. Six condoms!

He knelt on the bed, making the mattress dip. His fingers clasped her ankle and he dragged her towards him. 'We've got a lot of catching up to do,' he said. The hooded look he gave her carried both promise and threat now.

Her time was up.

Kate debated her options—fight, flight or surrender—for about two seconds. Then accepted the inevitable as strong, insistent fingers stroked up her legs.

'Anything you say, oh, lord and master,' she said, batting her eyelids.

She laughed at his surprised expression, then gasped as he hooked a finger in her knickers and ripped them down. He cupped her and her hips lifted instinctively.

'Good to know you finally figured out who the lord and master is around here,' he said, chuckling.

Drawing his fingers through the moist folds of her sex, he circled her clitoris. A lightning bolt shimmered through her body. She bit her lip, fighting to hold back her climax. Writhing away from his probing fingers, she got onto her knees, reached blindly for the waistband of his boxers. She might have given up the fight, but she intended to go down swinging.

But as she leant forward he cradled her breasts in warm palms, his thumbs stroking the engorged nipples. She moaned—and completely lost track of what she was doing.

He bent his head, nuzzled her neck. 'Keep going, honey, you've only just started.'

A pithy response to his teasing came to her lips, but she couldn't catch her breath as his teeth bit into her earlobe and his fingers plucked at her nipples.

She pushed frantically at the waistband of his boxers, struggled to free his powerful erection as the flames blazed down from her breasts to her core.

She stared at the magnificent column, then wrapped her fingers round the thick, solid length. She drew her hand up and touched the drop of moisture at the tip. His penis leapt in her hand and he groaned.

'You still owe me those Calvins,' she whispered.

He looked at her, his sensual smile tempered by the intensity in his eyes. Getting off the bed, he took them off and handed them to her. 'About time, too,' she said, then flicked them over her shoulder and reached for his penis again. He grabbed her wrist, held her hand away, his smile strained. 'No, you don't.'

He pulled her arm above her head, forcing her to lie back on the bed, and then settled beside her. She reached for him with her other arm, but he simply caught that wrist too, held both hands above her head.

'Remember who's boss,' he said, his free hand caressing the curve of her hip as if to emphasise his mastery over her.

She bucked beneath him, but he only chuckled.

'Let me go—this is silly,' she cried. 'I want to touch you, too.'

His teeth nipped her bottom lip. 'Not yet.' She could feel him, hard and ready, prodding her thigh.

'Why not yet?' Desperation edged her voice.

'Because I want to savour you.'

What about what I want? she almost shouted, but then his fingers delved into her sex, found the pulsing nub of her clitoris, circled it and then stroked. She shattered, the vicious climax exploding inside her. Her cries of fulfilment echoed in her ears as she convulsed against him, letting the long-denied orgasm rip through her with the force and fury of a hurricane.

Zack released her wrists and took in the beauty of Kate's face, soft and serene with afterglow. Her lithe, lush body was still shuddering in the aftermath of her climax. The pounding need to have her made him ache, but right alongside it was the fierce surge of possessiveness and pride and the underlying thread of fear. He'd never seen anything more incredible in his entire life.

He'd intended to prove he could take it slow, wanted to show that he could handle her as he'd handled every other woman before her. As a child he'd been a victim of his emotions. He'd never wanted to feel that way again. He had never considered that returning to The Grange might bring those feelings back. But it had. Kate's lusty, quickfire response to him only made him feel more exposed, more needy. And so he'd forced himself to step back, to prove he was the one calling the shots in this relationship. But his driving need to control her, control himself, had backfired spectacularly.

He wanted her now more than ever.

What if he could never get enough of her?

Shoving the disturbing thought aside, he gripped her hips, rolled onto his back and pulled her on top of him. Her fragrant curls curtained across his face as she braced her hands on either side of his head and smiled down at him, that overblown mouth of hers making him crazy. She sat up, straddling him. The moist heat cradling his engorged penis threatened to send him shooting over the edge before he'd even got inside her.

He adjusted her weight, trying to ease the torturous pressure while he grappled with the packet of condoms. But as he ripped at the foil packet, she lifted up and shimmied down his legs.

'No need to rush, Zack,' she murmured, her breath cool on his heated flesh as she nibbled kisses across his collarbone, 'because as it happens…' her tongue found his nipple and his blood throbbed harder in his groin '…I really want to savour you now.'

He cursed as her lips shimmered across his abdomen. Tantalising him, torturing him. His breath came in harsh pants as he fumbled with the condom. He couldn't think, couldn't feel anything except the soft sultry licks, the delicious torment. Then her tongue touched the head of his penis. The moist pressure speared through him like lightning and he shot upright.

'Stop it.' He grasped her head in his hands, his whole body shaking with the battle to control himself. 'Not like that. Not this time,' he said, hearing the alarm in his own voice.

She started to protest, but he took hold of her shoulders,

pulled her up and rolled over again. Trapping her under him, he covered her mouth with his, swallowing her words as he sheathed himself with the condom.

He settled between her thighs and, gripping her buttocks, thrust into her, making her take all of him. She was so tight, so hot, he could feel the rapid beats of her heart as her muscles clenched around him. He gritted his teeth, struggled to hold on to that last thin thread of control. He pumped violently, hearing her gasping sobs as he forced her to orgasm. Then his control shattered, and the surge of his own climax gripped him in a mighty fist and pounded him into bloody pulp.

Kate felt as if she'd been in a war. Her breath shuddered out in ragged gasps while her heart kicked in her chest. The aftermath of an earth-shattering climax swept through her blood like brush fire.

Zack flopped back onto the bed and draped his forearm over his eyes.

She studied him, feeling stunned and wary. What had just happened?

As her breathing finally evened out she propped herself up on an elbow and stared down at him. Short locks of dark hair damp with sweat clung to his forehead. She brushed them aside, drew her finger down his cheek and laid her palm on his chest. She could feel the staggered rise and fall of his breathing. He'd lost control, she'd made him lose control and the realisation had excited her beyond belief. But it frightened her too.

During their first night together the sex had been fun, carefree. This time there had been an urgency, an intimacy that hadn't been there before. It terrified her.

'That's what I call a game of strip poker,' she murmured, trying to keep her voice light.

Zack drew his arm down and looked at her. His lips curved in a lazy smile, but Kate wasn't fooled; his heart still raced beneath her palm. 'You okay?' he asked as his hand curled round her bottom, gave it a possessive squeeze. 'I was kind of rough at the end.'

'Don't be silly, I'm great,' she said, trying to persuade herself it was true. The tenderness, the longing she felt was just an extreme case of afterglow.

She pulled the sheet up, determined to ignore the emotion tightening her chest. She shouldn't feel this content, this complete. All they'd shared was good sex. Okay, stupendous sex. She turned on to her side away from Zack, feeling disorientated.

He lifted the satin cover over them, then his hands smoothed across her abdomen and he pulled her against him. 'Come here,' he whispered against her hair as his big body enveloped hers. His chest pressed against her back, the hair of his legs bristled against her thighs and she could feel the distinct outline of his penis still semi-hard and snug against her bottom.

Kate tried to shift away but his arms only tightened. Normally, she didn't cuddle after sex. She didn't like it. It felt too intimate. She ought to tell him so, but while she was debating what to say the sound of his breathing slowed, deepened and the possessive hand cupping her breast relaxed in sleep.

She yawned and her own eyelids drifted closed. She snuggled deeper into his embrace, her limbs suddenly unbearably heavy. Maybe she'd have a quick nap. She'd move away from him in a little bit, she reasoned dully.

Zack woke her twice during the night, driving her to new heights of sexual pleasure. But when Kate awakened in the morning she was still cradled in his arms.

CHAPTER FOURTEEN

'I SHOULD HAVE a word with your boss, young lady. Boudreaux works you too damn hard.'

Kate covered another jaw-breaking yawn with the back of her hand as Harold Westchester scowled at her. She'd been shadowing him for the last few days to write a report on The Grange's current operating practices. They'd hit it off instantly, but this wasn't the first time Hal had noticed how tired she was.

'Really, I'm fine,' she said, stifling another yawn.

'You two working late again last night?' the elderly hotelier asked.

The blush blossomed in Kate's cheeks. Well, that was one way of putting it.

Since their strip-poker night, Zack had proved to be a demanding boss and an even more demanding lover. And Kate had met every demand with lusty enthusiasm. But while Zack seemed to be able to operate on next to no sleep, she was starting to flag. Tonight, she had to tell him she needed a rest. Her work was starting to suffer. She might be sleeping with the boss, but she had no intention of slacking off on her job. But satisfying Zack's sexual appetite, as well as fulfilling all her duties as his PA, was exhausting her.

'We weren't up all that late,' she said.

Hal's eyes narrowed. He wasn't buying it. 'If you turn up here tomorrow yawning again, I'll have something to say to Boudreaux about it. You can tell him that from me.'

Kate nodded, feeling touched that Hal would be so protective of her. But it wasn't the first time he'd said something snarky about Zack. She put her notebook down on his desk. 'Why don't you like Zack?'

He didn't seem perturbed by the question. 'Don't like him or dislike him. I don't know him,' Hal said. 'And that bothers me. I'm not sure I trust him.'

Kate had suspected as much since her first meeting with Hal. That Zack was still avoiding the old man and had made no attempt to resolve the situation bothered her. Maybe she could put some of Hal's fears to rest.

'Why don't you trust him?' she asked carefully. 'He's a well-respected businessman.'

'That's as may be, but I judge them how I see them,' Hal said belligerently. 'When The Phoenix started looking to buy my place, I did some enquiries of my own. I found out things about your boss that didn't sit right with me.'

'Such as?'

'He used to be a gambler. I don't like them.' Hal gave Kate a penetrating look. 'I knew a gambler over twenty years ago. A real nasty piece of work, this guy. Selfish, violent and ruthless as hell.' Hal sat back in his chair, his cheeks mottled red, his eyes sharp. 'I wasn't about to sell my place to a guy like that.'

'What made you change your mind?' she asked, taken aback by Hal's outburst.

He picked up his pen, tapped it on the desk. 'I went to visit Boudreaux's place in Vegas. Incognito, of course. I was pleased with what I found. I got to thinking maybe Boudreaux wasn't like the gambler I used to know, but just a man willing to take risks.' A self-satisfied smile softened Hal's face. 'And the final offer I got out of him didn't hurt.'

Kate laughed, wondering if Zack realised he'd met his match in Hal Westchester. Then something else he'd said came to mind. 'How did you know this gambler?' Could Hal be talking about Zack's father?

The smile disappeared. Hal sighed and eased himself out of his chair. 'It's a long story, and not a happy-ever-after one, either.' He walked slowly to the open terrace doors, stared out of them. For the first time since Kate had met him he looked every one of his sixty-five years.

'If you don't want to talk about it, I understand,' she said quietly, guilty at having brought back what was clearly a painful memory.

'You know, I haven't talked about what happened back then since Mary died.' Hal turned back to her, his eyes shadowed by grief. 'But you're a straight shooter and I like you. Maybe I need to talk about it. I don't know why, but it's been bugging me recently.'

She rose, walked to him. 'I'd be happy to listen.'

They settled at the wrought iron table on Hal's terrace and as the sea breeze ruffled Kate's hair she sipped the tea Hal ordered and listened to what he had to say. Once he'd finished the first sentence, she knew exactly who he was talking about.

'The guy I was telling you about had a little boy. They checked in here one summer and right away Mary noticed something wasn't right. The kid had these hollow eyes, his clothes were dirty and he was stick thin.' Hal put his teacup down, a wistful smile tugged at his lips. 'Mary kept badgering me about the boy. Why hadn't we seen his father since they arrived? Why did the kid never come out of the room? The cleaning service hadn't been able to get in for four days because the do-not-disturb sign was always out. Still I didn't pay it much mind until I caught the little scamp trying to steal from my till. The kid went wild, so I locked him in my office.

I was all ready to call the cops, but Mary stopped me. Insisted we go check the room. What we found…' Hal shook his head, the look of remembered horror making Kate's heartbeat skitter painfully in her chest. 'The father's bed hadn't even been slept in. He'd skipped out that first night and left the poor kid to fend for himself.'

'What happened?' Kate felt like a fraud for asking the question. Torn between telling Hal what she knew and not breaking a confidence to Zack.

'We kept him,' Hal said simply. 'He had terrible nightmares at first, and when Mary finally got him to have a bath she found bruises all over. The boy was smart as a whip too, but he couldn't read. It took a while, but eventually Billy began to trust us.' Hal smiled. 'Billy, that was his name. And after a while longer, he just became ours. Mary said, it all made sense, why we'd never had kids of our own. That Billy needed a family and we were it. I knew it was a dumb idea. We should have told the authorities. But Mary was so happy, and so was I. Watching him fill out, watching him lose that hollow look, it seemed worth the risk.' Hal paused, poured them both a fresh cup of tea. 'After he'd been with us about three months, I was giving him some book learning and he read his first full sentence. I told him how proud I was of him. He just crawled into my lap and held on. It was the first time he'd let me hug him.'

Kate could see the sheen of tears in the old man's eyes.

'Well—' he huffed out a breath '—I'm not ashamed to say I was a grown man and it got to me. It still does. I felt like a father that day.'

'Probably because you were,' Kate said, gently.

'It didn't last. The gambler came back.' Hal's voice deepened with anger. 'He'd called once, early on, couple days after we'd first discovered Billy. I told him what I thought of him and his parenting skills. He laughed. Told us we could keep the little brat for all he cared and hung up on me. I didn't think we'd ever see him again. But six months later, he turned up on our doorstep. Said he wanted his son back.' Hal's soft brown eyes hardened with fury. 'You want to know why?'

'Why?' Kate asked, sure she didn't want to hear the answer.

'The guy's luck had gone bad while he'd been away. He figured the kid was his good-luck charm.'

'That's hideous.' Kate felt disgust and fury churn in her own stomach. The picture Zack had tried to paint of his father was of a happy-go-lucky charmer who couldn't quite live up to his responsibilities—the man Hal described was nothing short of a monster.

'I had no intention of letting him take Billy,' Hal continued, the words brittle with anger. 'I'd never have willingly let him go back to that. But his father was younger and meaner and he knew how to fight dirty. He beat the crap out of me. Hit Mary too, slugged her across the face when she tried to hold on to Billy. The boy was crying, hysterical. I remember seeing the father slap the kid so hard his head snapped back. I tried to rise, but Mary held me down, weeping. She knew there was nothing we could do, and the more we tried, the worse it would be for Billy.'

Kate bit into her hand, hardly able to breathe round the boulder of outrage and agony in her throat. How had Zack endured this man's brutality? How had any of them?

'We never saw the boy again. It devastated Mary and I. We missed Billy something fierce, feared what had happened to him. We called the cops, but they never found a trace of them. Eventually we had to get on with our lives. It's the guilt I can't get over, though, even now.'

'What guilt?' Kate brushed the tears from her cheek. 'What have you got to be guilty about?' she demanded.

Hal stared at her, misery shadowing his face. 'We should never have kept him. If we'd turned the boy over to the authorities like we should have, his father wouldn't have been able to take him back. Billy would have been safe. We were selfish and he suffered because of it.'

Reaching across the table, Kate grasped Hal's hand, squeezed hard. 'You're wrong, Hal. So wrong. You gave that child something he'd never had. You gave him a home.' She wanted so badly to tell him who Zack was. Knowing she couldn't made her feel partly responsible for the old man's pain. 'You weren't selfish.' She sniffed, desperate to make him see how wrong he was. 'You did the right thing.'

'But—'

She squeezed harder. 'No buts, Hal. You can't blame yourself for another man's crime. The only villain was Billy's father.'

'Do you really think so?'

'I know so.' She let go of his hand, gave him a watery smile. If only she could tell him how she knew.

Hal's face brightened, his shoulders losing some of their stoop. 'Gosh.' Hal gave a half-laugh, scrubbed his hands down his face. 'Thanks for that. It's made me feel...' he shrugged '...I don't know—better somehow.'

'I'm so glad.'

'You're a good listener.' He patted her hand. 'I guess that's one of the skills of a great PA.'

'I suppose,' she said, her heart lightening at the affection on Hal's face.

No wonder Zack had fallen in love with this good, strong, loving man. She couldn't think of a better role model, a better father for any young boy. It was a tragedy Zack and Hal had been given so little time together, but it occurred to her that those six months had been enough to change Zack's life. He could have become like his father, but instead he'd become like Hal.

If only Hal knew how much he'd really done for that little boy.

She had to get Zack to tell Hal the truth.

* * *

After giving Hal a goodbye hug, Kate walked back through the hotel gardens and ran possible scenarios through her head. How and when to approach Zack. How to get him to talk about Hal again. How to persuade him to tell the old man who he was.

She steadfastly ignored the niggling voice in the back of her mind that whispered: Why are you getting involved in Zack's personal life? You and Zack are just casual lovers. This isn't any of your business.

She wouldn't worry about that now, she was on a mission.

CHAPTER FIFTEEN

'I CAN'T BELIEVE this is the slum Steinbeck wrote about.' Kate peered over the balcony of the Fisherman's Wharf restaurant into Monterey Bay. The afternoon sunshine glittered on the water and caught the shiny brass fittings of a luxury yacht bobbing next to functional fishing boats draped with netting. Kate grinned as she spotted the whiskered snout of an inquisitive seal. The crying of seagulls on the lookout for lunch filled the air but couldn't compete with the seal's hungry bark.

'It's clean and pretty,' she said wistfully, 'but not quite as colourful as I expected.'

Zack smiled at her across the table. He took off his sunglasses. Those killer green eyes sparkled with humour and affection. 'You're the only woman I've ever met who'd prefer to eat in a flophouse than a five-star restaurant,' he said, picking her hand up.

'I didn't say I'd prefer it.' Her belly fluttered pleasantly as he threaded their fingers together. 'If we'd eaten here in Steinbeck's day we would have got food poisoning.'

'My point exactly.' He chuckled.

As she watched him playing with her fingers Kate realised how much she had come to enjoy Zack's company, to depend on it even, in the last week. She knew it wasn't wise. But after the fabulous morning they'd spent browsing the brightly coloured curio shops along Fisherman's Wharf and visiting Monterey's awe-inspiring aquarium—not to mention the two glasses of Californian Chardonnay she'd polished off over lunch—she couldn't summon the will to care. She'd worry about it a week from now, when she was on her flight back to England and this all became an impossible romantic dream.

'So, you ready to hit some more shops yet—' he grinned, turning her hand over '—or do you want to go home for a nap?' He bussed her palm with his lips.

Her heart swooped in her chest at the casually intimate gesture. She dismissed the jolt to her system as lust, pure and simple. They hadn't indulged in their usual morning escapades today because she'd been so exhausted and she'd missed it.

'Why do I get the feeling your idea of a nap is liable to tire me out more?' she teased, determined not to read too much into the smouldering look he was giving her.

This was about sex, nothing more.

'You could be right about that,' he said, keeping his eyes on her as he signalled the waitress. 'Let's hit Cannery Row, then.'

As he asked for the bill the memory of how sweet he'd been that morning came back to her. He'd let her lie in, brought her breakfast in bed and had then insisted they took a day away from work so she could 'recharge her batteries', as he'd put it. Her heart squeezed as it had that morning and she curled her fingers into a fist in her lap.

Stop reading so much into it. He was just being a nice guy—and she had been almost comatose after burning the candle at both ends for days. The way he'd taken care of her didn't mean a thing. But it still bothered her that she'd enjoyed being pampered so much.

The waitress slid the bill onto their table and told them to 'have a nice day'.

Zack pulled his wallet out of his back pocket and began to

count out some bills. As usual he'd decided to pay the tab without consulting her. She ought to call him on it, but they'd already had several disagreements about what constituted a legitimate business expense since they'd arrived in California and Kate knew she wouldn't win.

Reluctantly she let it go this time and indulged the urge to study him instead. He hadn't bothered to shave today and the stubble on his chin, coupled with the T-shirt and faded Levis he had on, gave him a rakish, dangerous look even sexier than his usual smooth, commanding, captain of industry image. No wonder she was having trouble distinguishing reality from fantasy.

She needed a distraction before she gave in to her raging hormones and jumped him in broad daylight. Surely there couldn't be a better time to talk about Hal.

She gathered her courage, knowing what she was about to say might spoil the sexy, easygoing companionship between them. 'I had an interesting conversation with Hal yesterday.'

He stiffened slightly as he stuffed his wallet back into his jeans. 'Yeah?'

'About an abused and abandoned little boy named Billy who he's never been able to forget.'

He swore. 'Kate, I told you not to interfere.'

She pushed the hurt to one side. 'I didn't bring it up—he did. His version of events was a bit different to yours, though.'

'I don't care,' he said, shutting her out.

'Well, you should. He's never stopped worrying about you, you know.' She reached across the table, laid her hand over his. 'You should put his mind at rest. Don't you think you owe him that much?' It was a low blow and she knew it, but she had to try and make him see reason.

He pulled his hand out from under hers, stood up. 'I'm not talking about this now.'

She stood, too, thrusting her chin out. 'When are you going to talk about it, then?'

He gave a harsh laugh, shook his head in disbelief. 'You know, that's rich coming from you. The woman who's better protected than Fort Knox.'

'What's that supposed to mean?'

'How about I show you what it means?'

He didn't look angry any more; he looked determined. In Kate's experience that could be dangerous. 'Show me what?' she asked, warily.

'Uh-uh.' He tapped her nose. 'If you want to talk about Hal you'll have to come with me first. Then we'll see.'

Okay, this definitely did not sound good. 'We'll see is too vague.'

'Fine.' He held her upper arm, propelled her out of the restaurant with him. 'I promise we'll talk about Hal—' he shoved open the restaurant's door, guided her through '—after you've done something for me. That's the deal, take it or leave it.'

Kate's skin began to itch. Something definitely didn't feel right. What exactly was all this about? But then she thought of Hal. Good, kind, honest Hal who had a right to know about the little boy who still haunted him. Whatever Zack intended, she couldn't let Hal go on suffering because of Zack's obstinacy. 'I'll take it,' she said.

The itch instantly got worse.

Zack held on to Kate as they walked through the tourist Mecca of the once-rundown Cannery Row. Silversmiths and designer boutiques vied for attention with souvenir shops and candy booths. The eclectic mix might be more picturesque than in Steinbeck's day but Kate was wrong about the atmosphere. The tourists and the locals alike exuded the same happy-go-lucky air that Doc and his pals had done in Steinbeck's imagination. All except Kate, who was stiffer than a street light by his side.

He knew how much she hated being manoeuvred into things—and how hard she found it to relinquish control. Tough. He hated it too, but that hadn't stopped her sticking her cute little nose into his personal business.

He didn't want to talk about Hal. Hell, he didn't even want to think about Hal. The shame and guilt over what had happened the day JP had come back had haunted him for years afterwards. He'd become a wild and angry teenager, hating himself and living on the edge of his temper, until he'd found an outlet in the poker parlours of Europe. It had taken him too many more years to channel it into something genuinely productive. He was within weeks of finally burying that miserable part of his life for good. He didn't want to open that can of worms all over again.

But in the last few days, his perspective had changed. He still didn't want to risk telling Hal the truth, but he might be persuaded to do it, if he could get one thing in return. And that one thing was Kate's trust. He'd enjoyed the light, teasing nature of their relationship in the last week. Hell, the sex alone had been phenomenal. But it wasn't enough any more.

He could feel the curve of her hip beneath the linen of her dress, stroked his palm over the fabric. Even above the bustle of the crowd, he heard her breath hitch and smiled. Her response to him was so instant and so dramatic. Every night they made love with a violent passion that still staggered him. He frowned, his hand tightening around her waist—and afterwards she always tried to wriggle out of his arms. He never let her, of course, but each time she tried it made him want to hold her even closer.

And then there was her damn hang-up about money. He'd always enjoyed giving lavish gifts to the women he dated. He liked to show a woman she was appreciated. With Kate he'd never even broached the subject because he knew what her reaction would be. She'd even got huffy the last few days about what meals and services he was paying for, which was ridiculous. No way was he letting her pick up the tab on a business trip.

He guessed that non-materialistic side of her, that stubborn, unflinching independence, was one of the things that had captivated him at first. But there was independence and there was pigheadedness. And her arguments every time he paid for anything were starting to bug him. He knew it was all part of that invisible barrier she'd put up to stop him getting too close. The higher she built it, though, the more determined he became to knock it down.

The exclusive jewellery store he'd been looking for came into view at the end of the street. Taking his arm from around her waist, he clasped her hand and led her through the crowd.

'Where are we going?' she asked, her step slowing.

'It's a surprise,' he replied, tugging her along behind him.

Kate's heartbeat kicked up as Zack pulled her towards the seafront. She was more wary than ever now. She still hadn't been able to figure out what this was all about.

'I don't like surprises,' she said cautiously.

He glanced over his shoulder. 'Stop looking so scared,' he said with a quick grin. 'You'll like this one.'

She decided to reserve judgement on that as he marched off again, still hauling her along.

The old-fashioned frontage of the silversmiths' shop looked sedate and chic sandwiched between a powder-pink arts store and a sportswear emporium. The sign out front stated it was a supplier for the local designers, but Kate had barely had a chance to glance at the window display before Zack had pulled her inside. With the lighting dimmed, an old *Mamas and Papas* tune playing softly in the background and a young saleswoman the only other person in the shop, it was an oasis of calm and good taste from the seething swell of afternoon shoppers and tourists outside.

Her misgivings momentarily quashed by curiosity, Kate wandered over to a long glass cabinet. Her breath caught as she examined the exquisitely detailed and expertly crafted pieces on display. Silver dolphins cavorted on a charm bracelet carved in a sea swell motif. Tiny rubies winked red fire at her in a necklace intricately crafted from white-gold filigree.

'What do you think?' Zack's hand settled on the small of her back.

Kate eased out the breath she'd been holding. 'They're exquisite. You should buy some cufflinks or something.' She'd already spotted some beautiful ones.

He folded her hand in his. 'I've got something to show you.' He led her to the end of the case and pointed at a necklace laid out on black satin.

Kate's heartbeat pounded in her ears. Clusters of tiny freshwater pearls cascaded down from a series of interlinked waves fashioned from sterling silver. She imagined the hours the designer must have spent creating such an incredible piece. The pearls looked like teardrops falling from a savage sea. It made her think of the surf the day before on their private beach.

'Why don't you try it on?' Zack said next to her ear.

She touched the glass, unbearably tempted. 'I'd love to.' She stole a glance at the shop assistant who had kept a discreet distance. 'It seems a bit cheeky to put her to the trouble, though.'

'Don't worry about that,' he said. 'She's paid to go to the trouble.'

Spoken like a man who's never had to wait on anyone, Kate thought wryly. But just this once she wanted to forget about who she really was and pretend to be a woman who could afford something as exquisite as the necklace shimmering seductively at her.

Zack signalled the young woman, who was only too eager to get the pearls out of the display case.

'It's called Sea of Dreams,' the assistant said in hushed

tones as she draped the necklace around Kate's neck and clipped the clasp closed. The young woman picked up a mirror from behind the counter, angled it so that Kate could see her reflection. 'It looks sensational on you.'

Kate's hand came up to touch the pearls, which glowed warm against the skin of her cleavage. She noticed for the first time the delicate, painstakingly fashioned silver chains attaching the pearls to the necklace. 'It would look sensational on anyone,' Kate whispered.

'Let me see.' Zack turned her towards him. His eyes lowered to her breasts. He reached up and ran the pad of his thumb under the pearls. Her skin sizzled with awareness, her nipples pebbling into hard points as his eyes met hers. 'It suits you,' he said, his voice low and husky, the green of his eyes smoky with desire. 'You're beautiful, Kate.'

Desire and something far more dangerous made Kate's skin flush with colour.

Zack glanced at the shop assistant. 'Box it up. We'll take it now.'

'What?' Kate said, shock tightening her voice.

'Certainly, sir,' the young woman replied eagerly and began to unclasp the necklace. 'Will that be cash or charge?'

'Wait.' Kate flattened her hand on the necklace, pushing the pearls into her skin. 'You're not buying this.' Had he gone completely mad? He hadn't even asked the price.

'Charge,' he said to the assistant, ignoring Kate.

The woman took the necklace delicately from Kate's numbed fingers. 'I'll put it in its case for you, miss,' she said.

Kate watched her walk off, stunned. 'Zack, don't be ridiculous. I can't accept it.'

His lips quirked. 'It was made for you,' he said, as if she hadn't spoken. He stepped closer, ran a knuckle down her cheek. 'When we make love tonight,' he whispered, his fingers curling round her nape, 'I want you in nothing but those pearls.'

The erotic vision sent heat spiralling down to her core. She forced herself to step back, to let his hand fall away. 'I don't want it.'

She'd expected to see temper, had been more than prepared to meet it. But instead his gaze softened. He shook his head. 'Yes, you do. But you won't admit it.' He cupped her cheek in his palm, the gesture so gentle it made her ache. 'Why?'

'I…' The tenderness in his eyes almost had her blurting out the truth. She stopped, swallowed the words. She couldn't let him see how needy she was. It would give him too much power. 'It's too expensive.'

He dropped his hands to her shoulders, slid them down her bare arms. 'That's not why and you know it,' he said. 'I thought we had a deal.'

So this was what he had meant. He wanted her to expose herself, to let him delve into the rawest corner of her heart. To take that last little bit of control away from her. 'I can't…' She stood rigid, restraining the urge to step into his embrace. 'I need some air.' She tore herself away and rushed out of the shop.

She could see the young assistant staring at her as if she'd lost her mind. Maybe she had.

She weaved her way through the crowds to the sea rail that edged the wharf. Gripping it until her knuckles ached, she stared into the bay. The sun shone warm on her face, but chills shivered up her spine—a reminder of old demons she'd thought she'd conquered a long time ago.

She stood frozen in place, only jerked back to reality when Zack's palm rested on her hip. 'You ready to talk about it yet?'

She huffed out a breath. She might have guessed he wouldn't give up so easily.

The slow rub of his hand radiated heat, warming her at last. She spotted the bag he carried. 'You bought it?'

He nodded.

She wanted to be angry with him but somehow she just felt drained. And scared. And hopeless. Because she wanted to take his gift, and she knew she shouldn't. Zack was a rich man. A thousand dollar necklace probably didn't mean much more to him than a spray of flowers, but it would mean so much more to her.

'Kate, it's just a gift,' he said.

But it wasn't, not to her. And if she accepted it, she'd be giving something in return she could never get back.

'I want you to have it,' he continued. 'Why don't you trust me enough to take it?'

It's not you I don't trust. It's myself, Kate's mind screamed, the plaintive cry of a tern echoing the yearning in her heart. 'I don't want you spending loads of money on me.'

'Who hurt you? At least tell me that much.'

Tears burned her throat, welled in her eyes. She blinked them back, hoped he hadn't noticed. No such luck. He pulled a handkerchief out of his pocket. 'Here you go.'

She sniffed, took the square of linen, inhaled his scent as she wiped her eyes. 'I'm sorry,' she said, her voice hitching. 'I guess I'm still a bit tired and over-emotional.'

'Don't lie to me.' He tucked a finger under her chin, lifted her face. 'You don't have to.'

The compassion, the understanding in his gaze was her undoing. Her lips quivered and the tears flooded over, streaming down her cheeks like a river breaking its banks.

He tugged her against him, wrapped strong arms around her and held her tight. So tight she could hear the strong, solid beat of his heart, smell the woodsy aftershave he used and the clean scent of his worn T-shirt.

She clung on, unable to deny herself his strength, his support, any longer.

Eventually, she choked back the last of her tears. His hands were rubbing her back, making her feel secure and at the same time unbearably needy. She pulled back, embarrassed by the wet spot on his chest.

'I feel like an idiot.' She dabbed at the moisture with the hankie. 'I'm sorry.'

He stilled her hand, looked down at her. 'Now will you tell me why getting a pearl necklace makes you bawl your eyes out?'

She sent him a weak smile, wiped her cheeks. 'You must think I'm completely bonkers.'

'Well, no woman's ever reacted that way to a gift before.'

She gave a half-laugh. 'I'll bet.'

His hand rubbed a circle of warmth on her hip. 'Talk to me, Kate.'

She sighed, looked out across the bay. Would it be so terrible to tell him this much at least? 'My father sent me gifts. Every birthday, every Christmas, at the boarding-school he sent me to. Because he preferred me to stay there than to come home.' She blew out an unsteady breath. 'He called them his tokens of affection.' She laughed, but it sounded as hollow as she felt. 'Which is quite funny, seeing as he didn't even like me.'

Zack felt tension knot up his spine at the misery on her face and her desperate attempts to disguise it.

She pushed her hair back. 'You see how pathetic I am. I'm twenty-seven and I'm still obsessing about the fact that my daddy didn't love me.'

'How did you know he didn't love you?'

She leaned back against the rail, balled his handkerchief in her fist. 'Honestly, Zack. You don't really want to hear all this do you?'

'Hey, you know all about my miserable childhood,' he said, struggling to keep his voice light and undemanding.

She heaved a heavy sigh. 'I knew he didn't love me, because he told me.'

'You're kidding.' He couldn't hide his astonishment.

She gave a weak laugh. 'No, I'm not. He never wanted me. When I had to go and live with him, he made it clear I wasn't welcome and sent me straight off to boarding-school.'

'Why did you have to live with him?' he prompted.

She jerked a shoulder. 'When I was thirteen, my mum died and…' she paused, quickly masking the flash of anguish, of grief '…there was no one else. I hardly knew my father. He'd visited us over the years, to see my mother, but he'd never shown the slightest bit of interest in me.'

How could any father be uninterested in such a beautiful, vibrant young woman? Zack wondered, but didn't say so. He'd already figured there was a lot about her parents' relationship she wasn't saying.

'How did you feel about him?' he asked carefully.

I wanted him to love me. I wanted him to need me, Kate thought, but stopped herself from saying it. It would make her seem even more pathetic. She couldn't bear to let Zack know how little protection she had once had. Not now, when her defences were so low again.

'We were strangers. I didn't really feel anything for him.' Or at least she'd tried hard not to. 'By the time I was seventeen I'd finally figured out that would never change.'

'What did you do?'

'I left school and never saw him again.' She held on tight to the sea rail. The surf rippled lazily in the bay, the seagulls wheeled above, ready to swoop on any unwary fish, but all she could see was her father's uninterested face telling her he didn't care what she did.

'So that's why you're such a pain in the butt about your independence,' Zack said beside her, making her smile.

'Yes, it's very important to me. And that's why I don't like accepting gifts. Because there are usually strings attached.'

She thought she'd made her point, and convinced herself to stick to her guns. But when she saw the determination in his eyes she wasn't so sure.

'There are no strings attached here, Kate. You'll have to trust me on that. Just tell me one thing. Do you like the necklace?'

She shuddered out a breath. 'Yes, I do.' He reached into the gift bag, but she grasped his wrist, stopped his hand. 'Let me tell you another story from my childhood, Zack.' At least this one wasn't so raw, so revealing. 'When I was ten, I found a baby kitten in the gutter outside our mews cottage in Chelsea. I begged and begged my mother to let me keep it, and eventually she gave in.'

'So that pout was lethal even then,' he murmured, bending his head to give her a fleeting kiss.

She eased him back. 'The cat was feral. It shredded my mum's antique furniture, bit me so badly I had to have a tetanus shot and then ran off after a week.'

Zack chuckled. 'I won't bite you, I swear. Not unless you want me to.'

Kate huffed, charmed despite herself. 'For goodness' sake. Can't you see what I'm trying to say? This thing we've got is going exactly nowhere. We both know that. I don't want to accept your gifts. I don't want to need them.' Or you, she thought silently. Please don't make me need you.

Zack stroked his open palm down her hair, brushing the wayward wisps behind her ear. The gesture carried a tenderness that made Kate's heart plummet in her chest. This was just what she was afraid of. With one look, one touch, one simple gesture, he could shatter her defences. Make her want things she could never have. She couldn't risk offering her heart to another man who didn't want it. Didn't need it. It could very well destroy her.

She opened her mouth to protest, but he placed a finger on her lips. 'Shh.'

The kiss was soft and gentle and only frightened her more. A fresh tear streaked down her cheek. He lifted it off with his thumb. 'You know what? If that kitten had stuck around it would have found out what it was missing.'

'But…' She tried to stop her heart from plummeting even further, but she was very much afraid it was already in free fall.

'But nothing,' he said. 'I'm not making any guarantees. This is as new to me as it is to you. But it feels right at the moment and it feels good. I say we see where it takes us and enjoy the ride for as long as it lasts.'

When they made love that night, Kate let Zack fasten the pearls round her neck. She could feel the weight of them, cool and heavy against her fevered flesh, symbolising much more than they should as Zack brought her to a staggering orgasm.

As she lay anchored in his arms, listening to his slow, steady breathing and inhaling the musky scent of recent passion, Kate realised she no longer had the will to even try to pull out of his embrace.

And she hadn't managed to get him to talk about Hal as he'd promised. But as she drifted off to sleep she knew she couldn't afford to worry about Hal's heart any more; she was going to be too busy trying to protect her own. Even though she was afraid it was already far too late.

CHAPTER SIXTEEN

'THE GRANGE IS YOURS, young man.' Harold Westchester put the pen down on his desk and stood up to shake Zack's hand. 'Feels damn strange, thirty years of my life, gone in a single signature.'

'You drove a hard bargain,' Zack said, letting go of the old man's hand. Kate noticed the way his eyes didn't quite meet Hal's. 'The Grange is in safe hands,' he continued. 'We'll honour its tradition of good service and honest hospitality.'

Hal nodded. 'I know you will. You know, despite your past I think you're a man I can trust.'

Zack's eyebrow lifted. 'My past?'

'As I told Kate—' Hal inclined his head towards her '—I've never been real keen on gamblers.' He sighed and sat down. 'And I always had this dream I'd be able to hand the resort over to my son some day.'

Zack shifted in his seat. His Adam's apple bobbed as he swallowed. 'I didn't know you had children,' he said carefully.

This was much harder for him than he'd anticipated, Kate realised. Her heart went out to him, even though she knew it shouldn't. Couldn't he see he had to tell Hal the truth?

'I don't, not really.' The absent smile that wrinkled Hal's lips seemed desperately sad to Kate. 'There was a boy once. He was like a son to Mary and I. He couldn't stay, but I always had this dumb notion he'd come back one day.'

Zack tensed. Kate reached across and covered the clenched fist in his lap with her hand. His eyes whipped to hers.

Tell him. She shouted the words in her mind, willing him to understand. To her surprise, he turned his hand over in hers and held on. Then he looked at Hal.

'He did come back,' he murmured.

A lump of emotion formed in Kate's throat.

Hal's eyes fixed on Zack's face. He inclined his head. 'What did you say?'

'He did come back,' Zack said, louder this time. He let go of Kate's hand. 'I'm the kid you're talking about.'

'Damn.' Hal's eyes glazed with shock. 'I knew there was something about you. It bothered me right from the first time we met.' He searched Zack's face. 'You are. You're my Billy,' he said, finishing on a note of astonished wonder.

Zack scraped the chair back and stood up. 'I've got to go.' He gave a stiff nod and headed for the door.

Hal's shout stopped him in his tracks. 'Don't you run out on me, Billy. Not again.'

Zack's hand fisted on the door handle, but he didn't turn it. He rested his forehead on the wood, the air whooshing out of his lungs. 'I'm not Billy,' he said on a broken whisper. 'I never really was.'

'Of course you are.' A huge smile bloomed on Hal's face as he walked over to Zack. Kate gulped down tears. 'You should have told me who you were two years ago, son.' Hal chuckled. 'I would have given you the damn resort for nothing.'

Hal rested a gnarled hand on Zack's back. A tear spilled over Kate's lid as she saw Zack stiffen. 'I don't want it for nothing,' he muttered, the sound muffled against the door. 'I don't deserve it.' Finally he turned and Kate could see the remorse in his eyes. 'I should have contacted you years ago. To say I'm sorry. But I was too much of a coward.' His shoulder hitched. 'I guess I'm not as different from my old man as I thought.'

'You were never like him,' Hal said, his voice thick with emotion. 'And what have you got to be sorry about anyway?'

Zack gave his head a bitter shake. 'I hurt you. And Mary. I didn't mean to.'

Hal rested his hands on Zack's shoulders. 'You were a child and we loved you. What happened was never your fault.' So saying, he pulled Zack into a manly hug.

Zack's shoulders softened as he accepted the older man's embrace and Kate felt a lone teardrop run down her cheek. She wiped it away and bit her lip hard to stop herself from bursting into tears. Goodness, she'd cried more in the last few days than she had in years. She pushed the thought away, unwilling to analyse why Zack's actions had touched her so deeply. She had no real stake in this relationship, this reunion. Why did it feel as if she did?

Zack heaved a shuddering breath. Hal didn't hate him. The relief was so huge it made his knees feel a little shaky.

The scent of peppermint and sea salt—so different from the smell of cigarettes and whiskey that had always clung to Jean-Pierre—propelled Zack back to those few brief months in his childhood when he'd felt truly happy, truly secure. As Hal continued to hold him, to pat his back, the knot of guilt, of anger, that had been lodged inside him for more than two decades finally began to unravel.

Hal stepped back, patted Zack's arms one more time, then let go. His gaze roamed over him. 'You sure are a heck of a lot taller than I remember.'

Zack laughed. 'I grew,' he said, realising that his palms, which had been clammy with sweat moments before, were dry.

'I should leave you two alone,' Kate said, gently.

Zack looked past Hal to see her standing by the desk, tears shimmering on her lids. She walked to them and he took her hand, linking his fingers with hers. 'You don't have to,' he said.

She was the one who'd made this possible. If she hadn't come to California with him, he never would have got up the guts to tell Hal the truth.

'You guys have a lot of catching up to do,' she said, a smile of reassurance brightening her face. 'I'll be at the cottage if you need me.'

She released his hand and spoke to Hal. 'I'm so sorry I couldn't tell you who Zack was, but I couldn't break a confidence. I hope you can forgive me.'

The old man beamed back at her. 'No forgiveness necessary,' he said, lifting her hand to his lips.

Zack watched her leave the room. She'd be at the cottage if he needed her. It scared him to realise how much that meant.

'That's one beautiful woman, inside and out,' Hal said as the door closed behind Kate. 'She reminds me of Mary. She'll make some lucky man a fine wife one day.'

The bubble of contentment burst inside him. He didn't want to think of Kate belonging to anyone else.

'Let's sit down, son,' Hal said, directing him to two armchairs on the far side of his office. 'These old bones aren't as spry as they used to be,' he remarked, settling slowly into one of the chairs.

Zack sat in the other.

Hal chuckled. 'Boy, but it's good to see you.' He thumped Zack's knee. 'You've really made something of yourself. I'm proud of you.' The words pleased Zack more than he wanted to admit. 'And Kate's a treasure.'

Zack's mood faltered. He didn't want to talk about Kate.

'I'm surprised a good-looking young fella like you hasn't snapped her up. And not as your PA,' Hal continued, giving Zack a wistful smile. 'Why, if I was thirty years younger, I'd—'

'She's not *just* my PA,' Zack blurted out.

Hal's smile faded. 'You're dating her?' He gave Zack a sober look.

'Yeah, I guess.' Although Zack figured 'dating' was too tame a term to describe what he and Kate had been doing.

'But she works for you.' Hal shook his head.

Where had that accusatory look come from? Zack wondered.

'You disappoint me,' Hal added. 'Sounds to me like you're taking advantage of her.'

Zack shifted, feeling as if he were seated on an iron bar instead of the well-stuffed cushion. 'No, I'm not,' he said. Then the image of Kate's expression yesterday—vulnerable and scared, when she'd tried to refuse the necklace—slithered across Zack's memory. Why were his palms sweating again? He rubbed them on his trousers. 'The attraction is mutual.'

'You're her boss, son,' Hal said firmly. 'You have sex with her, you're taking advantage. However mutual the attraction.'

Zack's blood pressure spiked. 'It's not like that. It's not just sex,' he said, not sure why he was justifying himself.

'You saying you're in love with her?'

The muscles in Zack's spine went rigid, his palms got even damper and his pulse zipped into overdrive. 'I...' He hesitated, had to force the denial out. 'I never said that.'

Hal frowned. 'It's either love or it's just sex, Billy, there is no in between.'

'My name's Zack,' he snapped, feeling cornered.

'You'll have to forgive an old man,' Hal replied, unfazed by Zack's show of temper. 'You'll always be Billy to me.' Hal's eyes softened. 'So what is it?'

'What's what?'

'Are you in love with the girl or not?'

There it was again, that dumb question. Zack shot out of his chair, paced over to the parlour's open terrace doors, suddenly feeling like a caged animal. Tension vibrated through him. He shut his eyes, the scent of lavender and brine flowing in on the breeze suffocating him.

He pictured Kate's face. Comforting and compassionate when she'd held his hand a few minutes ago. Bright and defiant whenever they argued. Sexy enough to make his heart stop when they made love.

He wanted her, sure. But was he falling in love with her?

Over the last week he'd been pretty much cross-eyed with lust, but right along with it had been a surge of longing and bone-deep contentment he still didn't understand. After all, she was easily the most difficult, the most impossible woman he'd ever dated. She used her independence like a shield and never let him get away with anything. That her obstinacy thrilled him as much as it infuriated him probably meant he was losing his mind.

'You figured out the answer yet?' Hal asked, touching his shoulder.

Zack glanced round to see an 'I told you so' smugness in the old man's face. 'We're not in love with each other,' he said, frustration sharpening his voice. 'We're friends. Nothing more.'

And that was the way it was going to stay. He wasn't going to let his heart get ripped out and torn to shreds. He knew what it felt like, had known since he was eight years old. No way was he ever going to leave himself open to that again. If he'd learned one thing from JP, it was that love was for suckers.

'If you say so,' Hal said gently, interrupting Zack's thoughts. 'But she's my friend now, too. So I'm going to ask you a favour.'

'What is it?' Zack asked, warily.

'When you two get the passion out of your system—when you decide to let her go—I'll be expecting you to make sure she doesn't get hurt.'

Zack nodded, but the hair at the nape of his neck bristled. One thing was for damn sure. Kate wasn't out of his system yet—and until she was, he wasn't about to let her go anywhere.

CHAPTER SEVENTEEN

As KATE WALKED along the crushed rock pathway back to the cottage she inhaled the fresh resin scent of the Monterey pines and finally faced the truth.

She'd fallen hopelessly in love with Zack Boudreaux. Super-cool, super-confident, super-sexy Zack. Her boss, her lover and a man who would never, ever need her the way she needed him.

She'd made some pretty spectacular mistakes in her life up to now—trying to win her father's love, trusting Andrew the rat—but this was easily the most catastrophic one so far.

She'd feared the worst yesterday when she'd accepted his necklace. But she hadn't realised the full extent of her idiocy until she'd watched him stiff and vulnerable in Hal's arms and the wave of love, of longing, that had welled up inside her had left her feeling punch-drunk.

A plump quail and its chicks waddled out of the long pampas-grass in single file, scratching for seeds. Kate watched them cross the path. The sight didn't make her smile as it had the day before.

How could she have been such a fool? Hadn't she always promised herself she would never make the mistake of falling for someone who didn't love her? She'd seen what it had done for her mother—tied her for life to a man who had ended up destroying her. Of course, Zack was nothing like her father. He might be arrogant, ruthless even, but he wasn't cruel and manipulative. He'd been generous and caring in his own way, he'd even held her when she'd needed it. But she knew he didn't love her back. He'd never given her any indication that this meant more to him than a casual—and temporary—fling.

She opened the cottage door and walked through the living room, slanting her gaze away from the fireplace as the memory of their strip poker game assaulted her. She paused by the French doors, pushed them open. The bougainvillea and trumpet vines gave off a sweet perfume, making her feel like a princess in a tower. The rocky cliffs gilded with spring flowers and the drama of the dark blue sea below completed the enchanting spell.

Kate let go of the rail and stepped back from the edge. There she went dreaming again like some naïve teenager. She wasn't Rapunzel waiting for her prince. This wasn't a dream. It was an illusion, that was about to suck her in and destroy her. She'd always prided herself on her independence, her self-sufficiency. She needed to cling on to the last remnants of it now if she was going to survive this.

She had to protect herself. She gave a quiet huff of breath, felt her heart crack. Which meant not begging Zack for a commitment he couldn't give. She had made that mistake once before, with her father, and it had cost her dearly. She already knew Zack's rejection would cost her a great deal more.

Drawing her shoulders back, she walked through the cottage to the bedroom she'd been sharing with Zack. She dragged her suitcase out of the wardrobe with leaden arms and began gathering up the clothes scattered around the room. She pulled her clean undies out of the dresser, threw them in the case.

The first step to a stronger, more resilient, more self-aware Kate was a Kate who didn't give in to her rioting hormones. Starting now, she had to stop sleeping with Zack. After all, the incendiary sexual chemistry between them had got her into this fix in the first place. She zipped the lid shut and wheeled the case through the bathroom and into the smaller of the two bedrooms.

The fantasy was over. She lifted her case onto the bed's down comforter, flopped down beside it. She had to start facing reality.

She'd taken a gamble sleeping with the boss, but now she'd fallen in love with him all bets were off.

Two hours later, Zack skidded the Ferrari to a stop in the cottage's driveway and yanked on the handbrake. Ignoring the crisp wind and the darkening sky on the horizon, he left the top down and jumped out of the car. He felt revved up, excited about what the future held and no damn rain cloud was going to dampen his mood.

After spending an hour chatting to Hal—and taking the first tentative steps to reforging the bond they'd once shared—he'd gone for a drive to clear his head. And to plan what the hell he was going to do about Kate. It had taken him a while to calm down enough to think it through rationally—surely just a result of the emotional jolt from his reunion with Hal—but once he had, everything had fallen neatly into place.

He didn't love her, any more than she loved him, but what they had together was way too good to throw away. He adored her company, her companionship, even her smart mouth, and they made a fantastic team—both in business and in bed. The simple solution to the problem had hit him like a brick as he'd handled the powerful car through the heart-stopping scenery of Big Sur.

He'd make her his permanent PA.

She could work for him during the day and they could play together at night. It would be the perfect partnership with no messy emotional entanglements. Kate was the most practical, pragmatic woman he knew—right down to those proper knickers. She'd see the benefits and wouldn't be sidetracked by loads of dumb nonsense about true love. She valued her independence. She wouldn't need more from him than he was willing to give.

He whipped his key card through the cottage lock and flung the door open. 'Hey, Kate, where are you?'

Damn, he'd never been so excited about offering someone a job before. His blood pumped through his veins as he strode through the living room, making him feel more alive than ever.

His enthusiasm had dimmed, though, by the time he'd checked out the terrace, the bathroom and their bedroom and hadn't been able to find Kate. Where had she got to? She was supposed to be here, waiting for him, so he could tell her about the great new opportunity he was about to give her.

As he turned away from the bed, though, he noticed something that sent a chill skidding up his spine. Where was the silk camisole he'd stripped off her this morning while taking her back into bed? He turned in a slow circle. And where were the rest of her clothes? Walking over to the armoire, he pulled open the doors, saw the empty space where her suitcase should have been. Every last molecule of blood seemed to drain out of his head. He blinked, tried to focus past the roar in his ears, the panic ripping at his gut. He swore viciously, the obscenity slicing through the ominous stillness like a jagged blade. The room seemed to fold in around him, and suddenly he was eight years old again, waking up to find the bed beside him empty and his father gone. He tried to force the memory down, but the panic crawled up his chest and sank its teeth into his throat.

Calm down, damn it. She hasn't left you, she can't have.

Slamming the armoire door shut, he stormed through the living room and out onto the terrace, his hands fisting at his side. He whipped round as the flash of blonde caught his eye in the cove below.

He took a deep breath, eased it out. Finally the choking panic began to fade, but the bitter bile of temper rushed up to replace it.

He took the steps down to the beach, two at a time. If she ever scared him like that again she was going to regret it. And, anyhow, what the hell had she done with her stuff?

CHAPTER EIGHTEEN

KATE PERCHED ON the slab of grey granite and stared out at the Pacific Ocean. The timeless rhythm of white surf foamed around the rocks topping the dark, angry blue peaks. A chilly mist hung low as storm clouds frowned over the coastline.

Kate knew just how they felt.

She wrapped her arms round her knees and swallowed down the tears that had been tightening her throat ever since she'd decided her fling with Zack had to end. She had to shake this ridiculous melancholia before she saw him again. Carefree and flippant was how she'd decided to play it. He'd be irritated she didn't want to sleep with him any more, but he'd get over it. They had less than a week left in California. Surely she could hold out against him that long, now she knew how much was at stake.

The knowledge that the days to follow would be agony only made her more determined to keep things dignified. She must not break down in front of him. She mustn't let him know how she felt. Pride, after all, was the only thing she had left. She shut her eyes, pulled her skirt over her knees and hugged her shins as the first drop of rain splashed onto her cheek.

'What are you doing out here? It's about to pour.'

She looked round to see Zack jogging towards her across

the sand, devastatingly sexy in an open-necked shirt and black trousers. Why did he have to look so flipping irresistible? It wasn't fair.

She forced a smile onto her face, climbed off the rock. 'I fancied a walk.'

One black brow arched as he got closer and studied her face. A raindrop splattered down and clung to his lashes like a tear. 'What's wrong?' He wiped the moisture away. 'You look like you're about to cry.'

So much for carefree and flippant. She looked past him, her throat closing on the words she needed to say. 'We better go inside before we get soaked.' She tried to walk by him but he took her arm, pulled her round to face him.

'Where's your stuff?'

She shivered, his confrontational stance as much to blame as the spots of rain dampening the light sweater and skirt she wore. 'I've decided to move into the other bedroom.'

The emerald-green of his eyes darkened to match the ominous clouds overhead. 'What the hell for?'

She dipped her head—and felt the instinctive response at the sight of his chest outlined by the damp splotches on his shirt. This was exactly why she had to stand her ground. She was addicted to him. Her head came back up. 'I think we should stop sleeping together.'

'Yeah?' The single word sliced out. This wasn't irritation, Kate realised, but something much more volatile. 'Well, what if I don't?' he finished.

'Please, let's go inside?' she said, struggling for calm. Matching his temper with her own would only make the fire between them flare hotter. 'We're getting wet.'

He looked ready to argue, but then the rumble of thunder signalled a deluge that drenched them in seconds. But as they raced up the cliff steps he kept hold of her arm, only letting go once they were inside the cottage.

'Stay put. I'll get the towels,' he said, his voice now rigid with control.

She stood frozen in place as he stalked into the bedroom. The soft pat, pat, pat of rainwater dripping from her hair onto the floor galvanised her into action. She peeled off her soaked cotton sweater, clasping her arms over her chest as Zack walked back into the room, only too aware of her bra made transparent by the rain.

He'd taken off his shirt and was rubbing a towel across his chest. She swallowed, feeling the familiar flames burn hotter. Terrific. Now she would have to argue her case while they were both practically naked. Why couldn't anything in her life be easy?

'Here.' He threw her the extra towel he'd slung round his neck. His gaze slid down to her breasts, making the heat throb harder. She pulled the towel around her shoulders.

'I thought we could grab a shower together,' he said, his voice cool, but his gaze more penetrating than a laser beam. He leaned against the sofa and folded his arms, giving her a stiff smile. 'Then we'll talk about our sleeping arrangements.'

Kate felt indignation flare alongside the desire. He was trying to ride roughshod over her. Typical. Well, this time, finally, she was going to get her own way. Pheromones or no pheromones. She had to.

'I'll shower alone, thank you. And then I'd like to make a few calls. I'll be back in Britain at the end of the week and I need to line up a new job.'

He straightened, the smile wiped off his face. 'You're not going back to Britain. I'm giving you a permanent contract as my PA.'

'But…' The implication of what he'd said sank in. She bit into her bottom lip, forcing down the spurt of hope. She couldn't stay with him, however much she might want to. It would only make things harder in the end. 'Why are you offering me this now?'

'Isn't it obvious?' Zack dropped his arms and gripped the armrest, tilting his upper body towards her. 'You're doing a fantastic job.' His gaze intensified. 'And we make a great team.'

'I...I can't accept it,' she said on a shuddering breath, feeling her resolve dripping away like the raindrops from her hair.

'Don't be stupid.' He pushed away from the sofa, stepped close. His body heat felt almost as overwhelming as the force of his will. He stroked open palms up her arms. 'I'm offering a good salary.'

Her heart plunged as he pushed her wet hair back and framed her face.

'You'll have your independence.' He pressed his thumb against her bottom lip. 'If that's what's bothering you.'

She heaved out an unsteady breath.

'I want you with me,' he said, pushing the towel off her shoulders, throwing it away.

She shivered violently.

'You're cold,' he murmured, holding her steady. But she knew she wasn't. What she was was weak. He took her hand, led her across the living room. 'Let's get you warmed up.'

But as they walked towards the bathroom her dazed mind registered one thought. He was wrong. She wouldn't have her independence. Despite the salary he was offering, despite the trappings of independence, she would be little better than her mother. A woman who'd sacrificed her identity, her individuality, for a love that had never been real.

Clinging onto the thought, Kate tugged her hand out of Zack's. 'I'm not doing this. I'm not taking the job.'

'Why?' Temper still simmered in his eyes, but with it was confusion.

She drew in a deep breath, gathered her courage like a shield around her heart. 'Because you don't just want a PA, you want someone to share your bed. And I don't want to be your convenient bed partner any more.'

He gave a harsh laugh. 'You're not what I'd call convenient.' He stepped forward and she bumped back against the wall. 'And, anyhow, you're lying.' His hands grasped her hips, held her still. 'I know you want me.'

'Stop it, Zack.' She wriggled.

He dragged her against him. 'You want to know how I know?'

She flattened her hands against his chest. 'No, I don't.'

His big body held her back against the wall. 'Your eyes get this ring of violet around the iris when you're aroused.' He captured her chin in his hand when she tried to turn away. 'And your lips get plumper.' He bit her lower lip softly as his thumb and forefinger skimmed down her neck. 'Your breathing gets rapid.'

Her breath panted out in ragged gasps.

'And your nipples get so hard.' He cupped her breast, lifted it. 'It's like they're begging for my touch.' He bent his head, took the swollen peak into his mouth, the hot suction scalding her through the cold, wet lace.

She moaned, the sexual thrill spreading through her like wildfire. 'I can't. I can't do this.' She choked on the words, unable to hide the quiver of longing.

He lifted his head. 'Yes, you can.' His arm closed around her waist as one powerful thigh pushed between her legs, forcing them apart, and rubbed against her sex. 'Put your arms around my neck.'

The harsh demand sliced through the fog of arousal and her arms lifted of their own accord. She clung to him, feeling the press of his erection through his trousers. Her legs quivered as her insides melted, surrendering against her will.

His lips crushed hers as his hands pushed under her skirt and kneaded her buttocks. The swift, heady rush of heat had her fingers fisting in his hair. Her mind screamed at her to stop him, but her body wouldn't listen. Like a kamikaze moth dive-bombing into the flame she held his cheeks, dragged him closer. Her breath shuddered out and her eyes closed as their tongues tangled in a kiss full of hunger, heat and mutual demand.

His fingers ripped at her knickers and then plunged into her. She bucked, cried out, already on the verge of coming apart. Humiliated by her inability to resist him, she let go of him, pushed against the hard planes of his chest.

'Please.' She gasped. 'Don't. I can't.'

He reared back, his face fierce. 'Yes, you can. You're soaking wet.'

He cradled her head and took her mouth again. Stamping his claim on her. The tidal wave of desire was so strong she couldn't hold it back any longer. She trembled, sobbed with need as his thumb pressed against her swollen clitoris and stroked hard until she cried out her release.

Dazed by the strength of her orgasm, she watched as he pushed her bra up, suckled the engorged nipples. She writhed against him, the fire streaming down to her already aching sex. She heard the hiss of his zipper as he freed himself from his trousers.

'Open your eyes,' he ordered.

Her lids fluttered open to see him watching her, his eyes feverish with desire, his face harsh with demand. 'You're mine,' he said, his fingers digging into her hips as he lifted her. 'You hear me, Kate.' She was trapped against him, her legs wrapped around his waist. The blunt head of his penis pressed against the folds of her sex. 'Tell me you want me,' he said.

'I want you,' she whispered, her sanity overwhelmed by the need clawing inside her and clamouring for release.

He thrust inside her. The slickness of her recent climax eased his entry but still it was difficult, painful in its fullness. She sobbed, tried to buck him off, as she felt herself losing that last gossamer thread of control. That last tiny portion of self.

She shook her head from side to side. Struggled to deny

the sexual frenzy, but then he plunged deeper. The brutal pleasure intensified and she gave a moan of defeat.

'Shh,' he crooned. 'It'll be okay in a minute.' And then he was fully inside her, stretching her unbearably.

He began to move, the tormenting rhythm bumping the place inside her he knew would trigger her orgasm. It roared through her, forcing her over the edge and dragging her back up. She cried out, breaking into a billion quivering pieces. Ecstasy and agony made one in her quaking body. He shouted out his own release as he emptied inside her.

'Are you okay?' he asked softly, his breathing harsh, his penis still thick, still firm inside her.

She pushed against his shoulders. 'Let me go.' The tears misting her eyes, closing her throat, only humiliated her more. She'd let him do it again.

He pulled out of her in silence. She flinched, her sex tender as it released him. She pushed her bra down, her fingers trembling as she fumbled with her skirt. She willed herself to stop shaking, heard him refastening his trousers.

He touched her cheek, a tender smile on his lips, but she could see the triumph in his eyes. 'I'll get Monty to sort out a new contract when we get back to Vegas.'

The words hit her like an icy slap. The horrible truth of what she'd done, of what she'd let him do, dawned on her with shocking clarity. Her own body had betrayed her.

She lurched away from his touch. 'I won't sign it. And I'm not going to Vegas with you.' She scrambled away from him. 'I'm leaving. I'm leaving now,' she said frantically as she rushed towards the smaller bedroom.

'Come back here.' She heard the pained shout but kept on going.

She slammed the bedroom door shut, shame and heartbreak turning to smothering rage. Suddenly, she was as mad at him as she was with herself. She ignored the loud crash as the door flew open behind her and slapped back against the wall.

'What the hell has gotten into you?'

She unzipped her case, pulled out a new top, refusing to look at him. 'Apart from your insatiable penis, you mean?' The words were crude, ugly, but it was how she felt. He'd used her desire, her love, against her and part of her hated him for it.

'Stop it.' He ripped the blouse out of her grasp. 'You came apart in my arms in there and now you're acting like some outraged virgin.' His fingers fisted on her arm. 'What the hell is going on?'

'I've fallen in love with you.' She hurled the words at him. 'Now do you get it?' Humiliation turned the shout to a whisper.

'What?' His fingers released her, the look of shock and confusion on his face made the last of the anger drain away until all that was left was a grinding, lancing pain where her heart should have been.

'I love you. And that means I can't stay with you. As your PA, as your handy bed companion or as anything else.' She picked up her blouse, tugged it on, tried to button it with trembling fingers. 'I saw what it did to my mother. I won't let it happen to me.'

'For heaven's sake, Kate.' His fingers stroked her arm. 'You're not making any sense.'

She looked at him then, saw compassion and it almost undid her. 'You don't understand because you don't know what it's like. To love someone and have them not love you back.' She sniffed, wiped her eyes hastily with her fist. For goodness' sake don't cry now, not when you've finally got up the courage to tell him the truth.

'So your father didn't love your mother. What has that got to do with us?' he asked, sounding exasperated.

'She was his mistress, Zack. His kept woman. He paid for her clothes, her food, the house we lived in. She would beg him to marry her, to acknowledge me, but he wasn't interested, because the only thing he wanted from her was sex. He never wanted her love—and he didn't want mine either.'

'Damn, Kate. I'm sorry,' he said. He pushed the curls from her forehead. 'But I still don't see what all that's got to do with—'

She pressed her fingers to his lips, the hopelessness of the situation tearing her apart. 'I love you but you don't love me. Can't you see? In the end it's the same thing.'

'But I'm not like him. I'm offering you a good job. I'm not trying to turn you into my mistress.'

'Just answer me one question. Do you need me, Zack? Really need me?'

His brow furrowed as he dragged his fingers through his hair. She felt her heart splintering. 'I care about you,' he said cautiously. 'I want you—you know that.'

'It's not enough,' she said miserably.

He reached for her but she pulled away.

'You want me but you don't need me,' she said. 'You don't love me.' She hugged herself to try and stop the shaking. 'Every time you touch me, every time you hold me, every time we make love, knowing you don't will chip away another little piece of my self-confidence, another little piece of my self-respect, until I'll be just like her. Begging for scraps when I deserve a banquet.'

'Damn it, this is stupid. You're not seriously going to throw away everything we've got for the sake of a few dumb words.'

She felt her heart shatter. 'Please leave, Zack. I want to have a shower and get changed—and then I need to arrange things so I can leave.'

No way was she going anywhere tonight, or any night. But Zack could read the misery on her face and see the goose-bumps on her arms. She was emotionally distraught and she was shivering. He doubted he'd be able to talk any sense into her at the moment—and he didn't want her catching pneumonia.

'I need to get some dry clothes on myself.' He nodded towards the bathroom. 'Have your shower. Then we'll talk.'

'There's nothing left to talk about,' she said wearily.

They'd see about that, he thought as he walked out of the room. Frustration and panic burning like lava in his gut.

CHAPTER NINETEEN

'I'LL SEE YOU in twenty minutes. Yes, that's right, San Francisco airport.' Kate put the phone down, heard the annoyed huff from behind her.

Zack stood in the doorway to their bedroom, his hair still damp from his shower and furrowed into rows. His feet were bare and he wore the T-shirt and faded jeans she remembered from their date in Monterey. The day he'd bought her the necklace. The painful stab of memory was just one of many she would have to endure over the coming weeks.

He propped his shoulder against the door jamb. 'You're not going through with this,' he said with so little inflection in his voice she wanted to scream at him. It wasn't a question. It was an order. She bit back the angry words that hovered on her tongue, forced herself to remain calm. Hysterics would only make it worse.

'Yes, I am. I phoned Monty and he said he'd already wired my salary into my credit card account.'

He looked at her, his eyes giving nothing away.

'I know I haven't worked the full two weeks,' she continued, as conversationally as she could manage. 'So I'll repay you what I owe you as soon as I get home.'

He swore viciously. 'This isn't about the money or the

damn job.' He didn't look indifferent any more. 'You're not going anywhere.'

'Yes, I am.'

He walked towards her. She stood her ground.

'We just had sex without a condom. What if you get pregnant?'

Heat pumped into her cheeks. She hadn't even considered the possibility. 'I won't.'

'You're forgetting, we've been living together for the last week. I know you haven't had a period and I also know you're not on the pill. So that won't wash.'

'So what if I do get pregnant?' She thrust out her chin, forced her eyes to meet his. 'It wouldn't make any difference.'

He gave a hollow laugh. 'Think again. I'm not letting you out of my sight while you might be carrying my baby.'

'You haven't listened to a word I've said, have you, Zack?' She suddenly felt unbearably weary. Could he really understand so little about what she wanted, what she needed? 'I would never bring a child into the sort of relationship my parents had. I know what that's like.'

His eyes narrowed. 'You better not be talking about abortion.'

She hadn't been, but it hardly mattered now. 'This is all hypothetical, anyway. It doesn't change a thing.'

She glanced at her watch, struggled to keep her voice even. 'The cab's going to be here in fifteen minutes and I wanted to say goodbye to Hal before I go. If you'll excuse me.'

She tried to walk past him. He stepped into her path.

'You can't leave me.' The anger in his voice surprised her, but more shocking was the anguish swirling in his eyes.

'Please, Zack. Don't make this any harder than it already is.'

'I don't want to lose what we have.'

He cupped her cheek. She jerked away. 'All we ever really had was great sex. Believe me you can find another playmate.'

The tears she refused to shed clogged her throat. 'They'll be lining up round the block once I'm gone.'

He shook his head slowly. 'But they won't be you,' he said. Was that pain she'd seen in his eyes? Before she could be sure, he turned away, walked towards the terrace. He stopped at the French doors, his back to her, braced his hand against the frame and bowed his head.

'This is so damn hard,' he muttered.

He looked tense and defensive, reminding her of how he'd been during their meeting with Hal.

She stood behind him, her voice shaking. 'What are you trying to say, Zack?'

'I promised myself when I was eight years old that I'd never let this happen again.' He was still muttering, his back rigid as he looked out into the storm-shrouded sky. 'And now it has and there's not a damn thing I can do about it.'

He sounded so frustrated and so annoyed, but if there was even a slim chance, a slight hope—she let the feeling of anticipation rise like a star in her chest.

'I don't understand.'

He shot round, pinned her with his gaze. 'I'm saying I'm in love with you and it's all your fault.'

His fingers fisted on her arms and he held her upright as her knees gave way. He shook her, the emotional battle etched on his face. Her heart thumped so hard she was sure it was about to burst out of her chest. Could he be telling her the truth?

'I was rich beyond my wildest dreams,' he said, accusation weighing down every word. 'I didn't have to live on the turn of the cards any more. I was doing just fine. And then you come along in your bra and thong and ruin everything.' He sounded so angry. 'I need you so damn much, it scares me to death,' he said, his voice even harsher, but the truth shone in his eyes, lighting her from within.

'Welcome to the club,' she said softly, sniffing back tears

of joy. 'You happen to be the most arrogant, overbearing man I've ever met.' Her breath hitched as a smile curved her lips. 'And if I could have chosen someone to fall head over heels in love with there's no way on earth I would have picked you.'

He yanked her against him, wrapping his arms around her so tightly her breath gushed out. She could feel his heart, pounding sure and steady. She clutched at his back, wanting to mould herself to him.

Finally he touched his forehead to hers. 'What the hell are we going to do?' He sounded more confused than ever.

'We're going to love each other.' Wasn't it obvious?

He hugged her close, cursed softly. 'I'm so sorry, Kate.' The words shuddered out against her hair.

'What for?'

'For being such a damn coward. I didn't want to love you, didn't want to admit it, even to myself, because it hurt so much before.'

She pulled back, took his face in her hands. 'What do you mean, before?'

He put his hands over hers, drew them down. 'They were such good people and he hurt them. I hurt them.'

'It wasn't your fault. It was never your fault.'

He shook his head. 'You don't understand. Hal's eye was all swollen up, he had blood on his lip. And Mary was crying. I carried that picture in my head for years. I hated JP after that. And I hated myself, too. I went off the rails when he died. Gambling, living in the darkness, taking dumb risks to make an easy buck. Just like he did.' He sighed. 'I turned my life around, eventually. Thought I was finally free of him. But I wasn't.'

The self-loathing in his voice made her heart bleed for him. 'Why do you say that?'

'Because I was still living by his philosophy of life. Never be dumb enough to love anyone.'

'You're not living by that philosophy any more, though, are you?' she said smugly.

A wry smile curved his lips. 'No, I'm not.' He held her chin in his fingers, stroked his thumb down her cheek. 'I guess I've got a certain lady in her bra and thong to thank for that.'

'Don't sell yourself short, Zack.' She hugged him close, her love and commitment even stronger than before, if that were possible. 'You've got you to thank for that.'

His hands caressed her bottom and she felt the wonderfully predictable swell of his arousal against her belly. 'And anyway—' she smiled against his chest, lifted her face to his '—those were proper knickers.'

'So you keep saying.' He pulled her skirt aside, slipped warm fingers under the waistband of her panties.

She jumped at the intimate contact. 'What are you doing?'

'Just checking,' he said, chuckling as she melted in his hands.

EPILOGUE

'HOW'S THE BUMP?' Zack murmured against the back of Kate's head.

'The bump's fine.' She grinned as broad fingers caressed the slight swell of her belly through the satin of her bridal gown. 'Now keep your voice down. I don't want everyone thinking this is a shotgun wedding.'

Zack gave a wry chuckle as the heat tinted her cheeks. 'You know, until this morning I never knew you were such a scaredy-pants, Miss Proper Knickers.'

'That's Mrs Proper Knickers to you,' she said, loving the feel of him pressed against her back, and feeling too mellow to rise to the bait he'd been dangling since their little disagreement that morning.

After all, this was her wedding day and it had been picture perfect. She took in the gardens of The Grange, breathtaking in their summer glory, and the specially erected gazebo bedecked with flowers where she and Zack had said their vows only half an hour ago. She smiled at the sight of Monty and Stella, their live-wire son Joey, Hal and a few other carefully selected guests enjoying champagne and canapés in the bright sunshine while beyond the cliffs the waves crashed onto shore in their timeless, never-ceasing rhythm.

Not unlike the rhythm of Zack's heartbeat, which she could

sense matching her own in the summer stillness. This place and time had a raw, elemental beauty that she would hold in her heart for ever, much like the man behind her.

She'd decided to ignore the fact that he wouldn't stop goading her about her request not to announce the pregnancy yet. Even the thought of it made her blush.

For goodness' sake, they'd only been together for three months. She still wasn't quite over the shock of discovering she was pregnant in the first place. Telling everyone else was too much for her. What if people thought they were only getting married because of the baby? Of course, she'd mentioned all this to Zack this morning. He'd finally agreed to keep the news to himself, for today. But she'd known from the pained look on his face, he was just humouring a pregnant lady—and he was unlikely to let it drop for long.

His fingers spread out across her abdomen, rubbed the silky fabric. 'You're not going to be able to hide it much longer. And I still don't see what the big deal is anyway.'

She turned in his embrace, cradled his cheek. Good Lord, he looked gorgeous in the Armani suit he'd worn for the ceremony, especially now he'd taken off his tie and she could see his chest hair where he'd undone the first three buttons of his dress shirt. 'I know you don't,' she said. 'But for today I want it to be our secret.'

He frowned. 'You're not scared about the baby, are you?'

'Right down to my toes, but I'm excited too,' she added quickly as she saw his frown deepen. 'It's just, the last few months, there's been so much to take in.' She'd been floating on a cloud of heart-bursting love, mind-blowing passion and soul-deep contentment and her feet still hadn't touched the ground. She was beginning to realise they probably never would.

There'd been the job Zack had offered her, not just as his PA but as part of his management team. There'd been the stunning glass-and-wood house he'd bought just down the coast road from The Grange, plus the marriage proposal and the frantic arrangements for the wedding when he'd decided he couldn't wait. And then, last but by no means least, the confirmation a week ago that they were starting a family—rather sooner than they would have planned. All thrilling, all wonderful and all scary as hell.

'Don't be scared, Kate.' He brought her fingers to his lips. 'I found out a long time ago, you make the most of the cards you're dealt in life. I figure we've been dealt four aces. All we have to do now is sit back and play them slow.'

'Umm-hmm.' She nodded. Oh, God, she thought, I love this man so much, I'm even turned on by his poker analogies. She fluttered her eyelashes at him. 'Well, if you've dealt me more than one ace, honey, you're going to be in big trouble.'

He chuckled. Letting go of her hand, he rested his palm on her shoulder, skimmed his thumb down her throat. 'Are you saying you don't want a pair of babies, or trips?' he said. 'Just think how big you'd get.' His eyes dipped, following the path of his thumb as it outlined the curve of her breast, already swollen in pregnancy. Her nipples peaked against the snug satin of her bodice.

She huffed. 'What is it with guys and enormous boobs?' she said, trying to put some indignation into her voice although she was getting breathless.

'You look great pregnant,' he said, his voice so husky the heat built at her core. 'And it's not the size of your boobs, so much as the sensitivity.'

The flush spread up her chest and her nipples tightened even more as she recalled what had happened the night before when Zack had decided to test how sensitive her breasts had become.

He pressed his thumb against her nipple and the heat lanced downwards. She gasped and grabbed his wrist. 'Behave yourself, we happen to be in public—and it's the middle of the day.'

'Sweetheart.' He folded her into his arms, laughing. 'We're married now. Public displays of affection aren't just allowed, they're encouraged.'

'Is that so?' She grinned up at him.

'Yeah. Anyhow, I'm the boss and I say married guys are allowed to come on to their wives any time they want.'

'Who made you the boss?' she demanded, raising a coquettish eyebrow.

'I did,' he shot straight back at her.

'I may have to dispute that.'

He lowered his head, his breath feathering her lips. 'I was hoping you'd say that,' he murmured, before capturing her mouth.

She wrapped her arms around his neck, welcoming the invasion of his tongue and revelling in the heat of the kiss. She matched his need, his desire, with her own while every single thought flew right out of her head. Bar one.

When it feels this good, I don't care if he is the boss.

But she had no intention of telling him that.

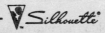

SPECIAL EDITION™

FROM *NEW YORK TIMES* BESTSELLING AUTHOR

LINDA LAEL MILLER

A STONE CREEK CHRISTMAS

Veterinarian Olivia O'Ballivan finds the animals in Stone Creek playing Cupid between her and Tanner Quinn. Even Tanner's daughter, Sophie, is eager to play matchmaker. With everyone conspiring against them and the holiday season fast approaching, Tanner and Olivia may just get everything they want for Christmas after all!

Available December 2008
wherever books are sold.

HARLEQUIN *Presents*

THE
MEDITERRANEAN
PRINCES

Playboy princes, island brides—
bedded and wedded by royal command!

Roman and Nico Magnati—
Mediterranean princes with undisputed
playboy reputations!

These powerfully commanding princes expect their
every command to be instantly obeyed—and they're not
afraid to use their well-practiced seduction to get want
they want, when they want it....

Available in October

HIS MAJESTY'S MISTRESS
by *Robyn Donald*
#2768

Don't miss the second story in Robyn's brilliant duet,
available next month!:

THE MEDITERRANEAN PRINCE'S
CAPTIVE VIRGIN
#2776

REQUEST YOUR FREE BOOKS!

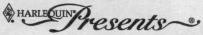 HARLEQUIN *Presents*®

2 FREE NOVELS PLUS 2 FREE GIFTS!

PASSION GUARANTEED SEDUCTION

YES! Please send me 2 FREE Harlequin Presents® novels and my 2 FREE gifts (gifts are worth about $10). After receiving them, if I don't wish to receive any more books, I can return the shipping statement marked "cancel". If I don't cancel, I will receive 6 brand-new novels every month and be billed just $4.05 per book in the U.S. or $4.74 per book in Canada, plus 25¢ shipping and handling per book and applicable taxes, if any*. That's a savings of close to 15% off the cover price! I understand that accepting the 2 free books and gifts places me under no obligation to buy anything. I can always return a shipment and cancel at any time. Even if I never buy another book, the two free books and gifts are mine to keep forever.

106 HDN ERRW 306 HDN ERRL

Name _____ (PLEASE PRINT)

Address _____ Apt. #

City _____ State/Prov. _____ Zip/Postal Code

Signature (if under 18, a parent or guardian must sign)

Mail to the Harlequin Reader Service:
IN U.S.A.: P.O. Box 1867, Buffalo, NY 14240-1867
IN CANADA: P.O. Box 609, Fort Erie, Ontario L2A 5X3

Not valid to current subscribers of Harlequin Presents books.

Want to try two free books from another line?
Call 1-800-873-8635 or visit www.morefreebooks.com.

* Terms and prices subject to change without notice. N.Y. residents add applicable sales tax. Canadian residents will be charged applicable provincial taxes and GST. Offer not valid in Quebec. This offer is limited to one order per household. All orders subject to approval. Credit or debit balances in a customer's account(s) may be offset by any other outstanding balance owed by or to the customer. Please allow 4 to 6 weeks for delivery. Offer available while quantities last.

Your Privacy: Harlequin Books is committed to protecting your privacy. Our Privacy Policy is available online at www.eHarlequin.com or upon request from the Reader Service. From time to time we make our lists of customers available to reputable third parties who may have a product or service of interest to you. If you would prefer we not share your name and address, please check here. ☐

HP08R

MEDITERRANEAN DOCTORS

Demanding, devoted and
drop-dead gorgeous—
These Latin doctors will
make your heart race!

Smolderingly sexy Mediterranean doctors

Saving lives by day…red-hot lovers by night

**Read these four Mediterranean Doctors stories
in this new collection by your favorite authors,
available in Presents EXTRA October 2008:**